HER VAMPIRE KNIGHT

INES JOHNSON

MIDNIGHT ROMANCE

CHAPTER 1

VIRIUS

I shiver as I run barefoot down the streets. My nostrils fill with the foul stench of refuse, both human and animal. But the smell makes my empty stomach grumble. It hasn't been filled in days. I don't let that stop me as I move through the carts and the people.

Pushing my body harder, I run down the footpaths. I leap taller than I am as I hop over a newly installed drainage ditch. Once, I would have marveled at the new age invention, but there is no time. I skirt a bridlepath, narrowly avoiding horse hooves.

Finally, I reach the door. The sounds of laughter barely mute the sound of squeals and grunts. I have only been alive for ten years, maybe less. No one paid me enough attention to keep track since my birth, and I hadn't learned my numbers until long after I'd learned to run. But even then I'd learned to keep my mouth shut. Any sums I kept, I kept in my head.

I stayed quiet with the butcher who cheated *Lena* Marcella. Neither truth nor a lie would have done me any good. Either a strapping would come from the butcher when the *lena*'s back was turned, or the *lena* would lash me if the madame of the house thought I'd stolen from her. I knew I couldn't win, so I kept silent and simply dealt with whatever punishments came.

It was all I could do. Slaves had no rights, no say in their own lives, or what their masters and mistresses did with their flesh.

"No, sir. Please, wait."

The squealing maiden is playing coy. I know because of the breathlessness in her voice and the fact that she's not running away from the large, out of shape male. His pockets are thick, and so she will stay and pretend to resist, as many of the rich men of Rome like. Others prefer for the women to seduce them so that they can deny their baser leanings and blame it on the *puella*s they've come to patronize.

This trick is especially used when the men come seeking out other males. Men enjoying the touch of others of their sex isn't so much as frowned upon in the streets of Rome as it is simply not discussed.

I pass by rooms where men pummel into women from behind. I peek into another where a woman has her head buried between a rich matron's thighs as the gray-haired, married woman trembles with delight. In another room, a man and a woman service a *praetor*. That particular magister runs his hands through the female *puella*'s hair but his gaze is locked on the male's bare member.

I finally reach the scene I ran all the way for. A large male has a woman cornered in an empty room. There is no bed here upon which to do one's business. The customer is fully clothed, unlike the other patrons of the establishment. But the *puella*'s back is bare. Her skin is blood red from the flailing of his instrument.

"Please," she begs.

Her voice isn't breathless in calculation or desire. She fights for breath with each word she is able to utter as the lash slices into her pale skin. The man digs his meaty paws into her blonde braids and yanks her head back.

"Please," she whimpers, barely audible as her neck strains and her wounds pulse.

There is no fight in her. She knows better. Though she doesn't want this, she has no choice. She is a slave. This man has paid for her time, to do with her as he wishes.

It isn't rape even though she says no. Slaves can't say no to the use of their bodies. The only person she could report this ill-use to is the madame. *Lena* Marcella would bother to take the matter to court if her property was damaged beyond repair. Which may be why the brute Felix keeps his lashing to the slave's back and not the place where her thighs split. Bright dots of red blood stain his alabaster skin.

I'd heard that Felix the albino was coming to the brothel. The man's name, along with his unnaturally pale skin, strikes horror into the hearts of anyone who sees him. He has been in town for a month and everyone in the brothels know of his name, his features, and his proclivities.

The albino has never ventured this far from the center of town. Not many come to this brothel on the outskirts. Vera is the prettiest *meretrix* in the establishment. When I heard Felix was coming in this direction, I knew he would come straight to her.

With Vera's skin rent and her spirit broken, Felix finally undoes the folds of his toga. Vera whimpers, but she does not resist. I cannot stand by any longer; I launch myself into the room.

The albino is bigger than me. Stronger than me. With a

weapon in his hand that is twice the length of me. But I can't allow him to keep up his assault. He doesn't even register when my fist hits his flesh.

"Virius, no," says Vera, with more strength in her voice than I thought possible. "Get out of here."

"No," I shout, launching another strike at the brute. "I'll save you, Mother."

My mother straightens on her elbows. Blood drips down her back as she does so. "Do not call me that," she hisses.

Vera's eyes glare into mine. We have the same face. The same mouth. The same eyes. But she doesn't claim me as hers. I'd often wondered if I came into her belly like this, by a man forcing his way into her. I later realized she likely didn't know who my father was as she'd been spreading her thighs for food and shelter since she was my age.

"Oh, look at that," trills a voice as gay as a bird's. "You have a valiant little knight."

I turn to the corner of the room. I hadn't noticed that there was a witness to Felix's brutality. A woman sits upon a cushioned chair.

Her beauty is beyond Vera's. She is something other-worldly. Her skin is pale, but not as translucent as Felix's. Her dark eyes tilt upward like a cat's. Her hair is long and white and hangs about her cherub-like face in a shimmering curtain. She smiles at me, and I am transfixed by her blood-red lips.

"He's nothing," says my mother, steel coming into her voice. "Send him away, and let's continue our fun."

But the woman's gaze is latched onto me. "A man who comes to a woman's rescue even though the odds are against him. Aren't you precious?"

"He does not need to beat her," I say. "She will lie with him willingly."

"But darling, it's the beating that will make her taste so sweet."

I know that sex is had not just with the parts between a person's legs but with the mouth as well. It was something else I cataloged away, as I knew this would be my life one day. Likely sooner rather than later, I would be filling my belly and keeping a roof over my head by lying on my back, bending over, and kneeling down. I was born a slave, the property of *Lena* Marcella to her most prized and highly paid *meretrix*.

"Don't worry about her, little one," says the white-haired woman. "She won't remember a thing when she wakes up. But you... I think I'll take you with me. I've never had a pet."

She beckons me to her. I have not been taught that I have any choices. So, I go to her.

"N-no, wait."

I'm shocked that any sound of protest comes from my mother. But I do not glance back at her. The white-haired woman's gaze holds me transfixed.

"How much?" she says.

The silence in the room is so loud that I can hear the soft inhale from my mother's shock, and then her throat working as she swallows down any of the care she may have had for me as a child of her loins.

I do turn then, and I see my mother calculating. The blood on her back is ignored. The open wounds are forgotten. She names a sum.

"Done." The white-haired woman turns my face back to hers. "Wait outside, darling knight."

I look at my mother, but she isn't looking at me any longer. Her eyes have glazed over in that look the *puellas* get when they have a particularly hard client to deal with. Felix goes back to his toga folds. He drops the flail and removes the instrument between his thighs. I see a flash of sharp teeth as he looks down at the blood on my mother's back.

There's a crack against my face. I have been slapped before. Never before have I seen stars behind my eyelids. I open my eyes to find the white-haired goddess looking down at me as though a demon lives behind her dark gaze.

"Outside, I said. You belong to me now, and I do not take any disobedience."

I am shoved out the door on unsteady legs. When the door slams shut, all I hear are the sounds of a man grunting. Then I hear my mother scream.

My eyes snap awake as I go from the nightmare of my youth to the present day. Four hundred years later, and the pain is still raw in my chest. But it's not my mother I see looking down at me in the corner. It's not my sire who made my life a misery for two centuries.

In the corner sits a woman with fire in her eyes. She stares not at my dick, which has for centuries been the only thing of use on me to women. She stares at my mouth. I can't tell if it's because she wants to lick my fangs, or if she is contemplating ripping them out.

I am no longer a slave. I am no longer a boy. I could snap this woman's neck with little effort. But I'm curious to know what she desires of me. Because for the first time in my centuries of a half-life, the desire is returned.

CHAPTER 2

ZAHARA

I stare at the beast's body as he stirs from his day's long sleep. He's not hairy like many of the four-legged prey I've hunted in the rainforests of Central America. But he is the biggest game I've taken down. Because Virius Serrano is a big male.

One of his arms is thrown over his forehead, holding back his thick blond curls. His other hand is flung out to the side, fingers flexing and curling as though lying in wait for a would-be attacker to come upon him. Little does he know he is already caught.

He walked into my trap just a half-day ago. In fact, he willingly offered himself up to me in exchange for his brother's life. I'd say it was an honorable move, but I know better. There is no honor in the still hearts of vampires.

My gaze remains transfixed on my quarry. Virius wears a t-shirt featuring the Sioux warrior Crazy Horse. On his strong thighs, he wears cowboy chaps over the jeans that are molded to his form.

I take my time as my gaze takes in his package. Not because I find his form pleasing. I find the whole get-up offensive. Cowboys and Indians, really?

My father's people are of the Tohono Oodom tribe. My mother hails from the ancient Maya of Central America. It's not my indigenous tailfeathers that are ruffled. What flutters through my head like a butterfly flapping its wings on its nascent flight is how the man's chest fills out his shirt.

With each inhale, the hem of the t-shirt rises up higher and higher, giving me a view of the man's eight-pack. There is a tiny dusting of dark blond hair that extends from his belly button and disappears down the waistband of his jeans. The bulge there is clear through the fabric.

I'm supposed to make a baby with him.

The thought makes me cross my legs where I sit on the edge of the cot. The thought and the sight of the bulge in his pants are overwhelming. Yes, Virius Serrano is a very, very big boy.

I wouldn't call myself petite. But beside this golden-haired lion, I might as well be a house cat. I have no idea how this will work.

Yes, of course I know how sex works. I grew up around animals. I read a couple of romance novels. And I have Wi-Fi on my cell phone, though the little screen doesn't allow as much detail as I would like.

I know the mechanics of the textbook, step by step instructions. But I haven't followed the steps yet, mainly because none of the boys I grew up with would dare come near my sacred womb—or rather, my magical pussy as I started calling it after reading romance novels.

I place my hand over my flat belly. In just a few days' time, a baby will begin to grow in there. A child with even more responsibility than me. My womb is the vessel to break a curse.

I thought I'd had a rough time, being part American Indian and part Indigenous Mayan. Being raised with the traditional values of my people while lending an ear to modern feminist values. Being a human female with an animal living inside of her.

My unborn son will exist between two worlds as well. But his existence will be in the middle of two supernatural worlds. My son will be part jaguar shifter and part vampire.

There has never been such a pairing. It is completely unfathomable. But it was prophesied, and that prophecy is due to come to fruition in just a few nights.

In just a few nights, I will have to take this big man into my body. Have him move inside me like I've seen animals do in the field, pictures in textbooks, couples in movies.

I huff out an impatient breath. I've waited twenty-two years for this moment. All this build-up for nearly two decades. Then, in a matter of a couple of days, it will be over in a few moments, if the animals' couplings have taught me anything.

As though he could hear my thoughts, Virius jolts awake. His gaze immediately tracks to mine. Those honey-colored eyes hold me in place, leaving me in a situation I have never faced in my entire life. His gaze makes me feel as though I am the caught prey.

Which is ridiculous. He's my captive. He's about to bend to my will.

And then all I can think of is bending. Him bending me over and taking me from behind as I've seen it done in nature.

Virius's blond brow lifts. In amusement? In challenge? In acceptance?

I have the presence of mind to blush. Vampires can get

into people's heads. Has he seen what I've been thinking about him?

His lips part. The top one, shaped in the bending curve of a heart, loosens from the lush bottom one. That bottom lip looks like the plumpest pillow I've ever seen. I want to lay my mouth against it—that is, until I see the bright gleam of fangs.

I shift on the cot, crouching into a fighting stance. A dagger is in my palm.

"I'm sorry," he says.

His voice is like the low grumble of a lion. I would have thought he was roaring at me before charging and taking me with those pointed teeth. The more shocking move is that I hold still.

Not because I want him to bite me, but because I've never before heard the words he's said; definitely not from a male.

"Did you just apologize?" I ask, not lowering my blade.

Virius takes a deep breath. He rubs his hands over his face, closing his eyes and leaning his head back. His jugular is exposed. He's presenting the most sensitive part of himself to my blade as though he isn't in the least afraid of me. When he pulls his hand away and straightens his head, the fangs are gone.

"I would never do anything to harm you, Zahara," he says.

It's the first time he's said my name. The way he forms the Z makes it trill like a string pulled on a guitar. It hums through me, making me vibrate until it reaches the R in my name. That becomes a caress that pulsates all the way down to my fingertips and toes.

He holds me still once more with those eyes. They shine so brightly that I can see everything in him. Does the man not know how to shutter his gaze? The eyes are truly the window to the soul, and he has left the door wide open for me.

Or maybe it's a trick. Maybe he's trying to mesmerize me. I blink and look away. But I still feel drawn to him, wanting to look back up and seek the heat of his gaze.

"I'm sorry that I had to sleep," he says. "The sun's pull on me is too great. I fought as long as I could to stay awake and protect you."

Protect me? "You do realize that you're a captive here?"

He looks around the room as though it's the first time he's seeing it. The rumors about him all indicate that Virius... isn't quite right in the head. Something about the vampire who turned him being a sadistic Dominatrix from the old world.

"I'm holding you captive," I say slowly. "So, I don't need your protection. You're under mine."

Virius grins at that. For a creature who is allergic to the sun, his smile would be that star's greatest rival. "You are wee but mighty."

He called me that the other day.

Wee.

Like he's some Scottish highlander and I'm his lass.

I know he was a Roman soldier who'd later gotten his kicks in the Spanish Inquisition by first torturing and then drinking the blood of prisoners. And now he is squatting on my family's ancestral land. But once I am with child, the gods will see fit to right that wrong the American government thought they could erase with paper and pen. Which means there is no time like the present to get down to business.

"Listen, here's the deal," I say. "I'm holding you here until the eclipse, which is in a couple of days."

Virius nods, but I get the feeling he's not listening. His gaze is on my lips. His golden gaze flitting up, down, and across as I form words.

11

Subconsciously, I wet them. The tip of my tongue sneaks out and curls over my top lip. At the move, his nostrils flare. Something inside me heats, making my next words easy to say.

"We're going to have sex then. On the night of the eclipse."

Virius blinks. Then he frowns. He had been leaning slightly forward, towards me. Now he leans back, as far away from me as he can get.

That doesn't seem right. I'm sure he's into me. Most guys are into me. If they're not from my tribe, they look at me like I'm some exotic, brown treat they want to go slumming with.

Not Virius. He looks horrified at the thought of getting busy with me. Maybe vampires are immune to the magic sparking between my thighs?

"It's not my idea," I hurry to say. My wounded pride is doing backflips to put some distance between us. "It's part of the prophecy."

The prophecy that will break the curse of the land and return its rightful ownership to my people. Not that I truly care about that.

I mean, of course I want to claim my birthright. But what I want more is to stay here in the States. Arizona has nothing on the beauty of Guatemala's rainforest. But the educational opportunities of these northerners are something that makes my mouth water.

"Is someone forcing you?" Virius asks, his voice going to a low register that warns of danger.

I like the way it rumbles through me. It coils and uncoils like a snake. The weight of it wraps around me, and something inside of me shivers.

"Because I will pull out his entrails through his arse and feed them to the bastard."

Well, that was certainly visual. At least I see that Virius's distaste has less to do with me than with the thought that I may be in danger.

"No," I say. "No one's forcing me. It's my destiny."

"Your destiny?"

"Yes."

Virius considers that. The hand he raked through his hair now scratches at the day's worth of stubble on his chin. "My answer is still no."

The dagger I forgot I was holding slips from my grasp. It clatters on the bed with a thud, resting between us. "No?" I ask.

"No," he confirms. "I will not have sex with you."

So, let me get this straight: I'm finally about to bag a guy who is not in my tribe, who doesn't look at my vagina like it's the holy grail, and he's telling me no?

Hunh?

Maybe I'm the one who is cursed.

CHAPTER 3

VIRIUS

I've *known* many women over my life. Thousands upon thousands. Though I haven't seen many of their actual faces. My memories of the women I've fucked are all of their cunts and asses.

All those pussies were pink; only the shade differed. Each woman's pussy had two lips that split open as they grinned at my cock. Some lips were full and plump. Others were flat and saggy. Not all came with a pearl at the center. Some had been mutilated due to sacred rites of gods or legal rights of men.

None of these women cared to see my face. Each cunt came to me for one purpose only: to be filled and stretched by the monster that prowls between my thighs.

For nearly two centuries the beast below has lain in a quiet slumber, rarely stirring. I haven't been forced to fuck since Domitia walked into the sun. I do not seek pleasure with my hand, not having the desires that normal males do. And so, it slept.

Until just this moment. Until Zahara called to it with those pretty lips of hers.

For the first time in nearly two hundred years, the beast lifts its head. The massive twin sacks it rests between stir. A bead of interest forms, dripping from the single eye of the twisted creature hidden in my pants.

"I will not have sex with you," I say again.

My dick pulses, calling me a liar. It has always been the only part of my body that ignores the fact that I do not lie. It has fucked women time and again—against my will. All at the behest of the one who changed me into the blood-sucking whore that I am.

My mind was rarely interested in the cunts and asses and mouths open to my cock. My thoughts and needs were just as irrelevant to my cock as they were to Domitia. If Domitia presented me with the bared orifice of a paying client, my dick would get hard.

Most of the time. When my dick didn't rise to the occasion... Well, then Domitia had her ways.

I was her slave. She owned my body. It was at her command.

I got off easier than my brother Hadrian. Luckily, all our sire wanted of me was my dick. She'd ripped Hadrian's heart out—more than once.

"Are you saying you don't want to fuck me?"

I want to growl at the foul words coming out of Zahara's perfect mouth. Her lips are pink, a deep ruddy pink. There is a divot at the center of her top lip. A small pearl that I want to taste. My fangs sharpen, knowing that the flesh of her mouth is filled with her blood. At the same time, the blood I have in me rushes southward, answering the call of the beast.

"No, little one, I am not going to fuck you."

Once again, my dick calls me a liar. It throbs in my pants, ready to take a bite out of the zipper that encases it behind the harsh cloth. It wants to get at Zahara. To get inside her. The lush lips of her face would be a perfect place to break two centuries of celibacy.

The hell I'll ever let that monster out. I would die before letting it ravage her. I press the heel of my hand over the beast to leash it.

Zahara's gaze tracks my movement, her dark eyes opening wider as she sees the impression of my cock against the fabric. The outline of my dick can be traced down my thigh. My hand is not large enough to cover my entire length.

"You see now," I say. "You're too small."

Zahara's plump lips curl into what I think she means to be disgust. Her brows pinch together. Her nose crinkles. Her lips purse. Like everything about her, I find the movements fascinating.

"Puh-lease," she scoffs. "Every man thinks his prick is the biggest."

"I don't *think*, little one. It's a fact. I am massively endowed. I would easily split you wide open."

There are many women who like that. Women who wanted to be stretched so far that they tore as I pounded into them. I knew my dick had done its job when they couldn't walk for days, sometimes weeks, after fucking my cock.

"I won't let it hurt you," I say to Zahara.

"You do know that the female body is made to shove out something the size of a watermelon?"

A watermelon? I've never heard of such used in sex. I've borne witness to women mounting horses. One even tried to fuck an elephant—to a fatal conclusion.

I don't think that is Zahara's aim. She doesn't strike me as a masochist. Or a size-queen who aches for the stretch of an oversized phallus.

"I'm not the width of a gourd," I say. "Definitely the length, though."

She snorts at that. Her lips lift the tiniest fraction. Is that a smile? I'm not sure. I have never made a woman smile without my dick being put to use by her.

Just like her scowl, Zahara's grin is beautiful, breathtaking. I need to remember what I did to make it happen so I can do it again. We were talking about my cock, and her vagina, and pushing fruit out of it. The idea of her vagina as a piece of fruit is definitely appetizing, both to my mouth as well as my cock.

"Like it or not," she says, "we are going to have to fuck."

I still don't like the foul words coming from her sweet mouth. But my dick does. It punches at the front of my pants again.

"It's the only way to break the curse," she says. "The only way to get our land back."

"Your land?"

"The Serrano vineyard is on sacred Tohono O'odham land." Zahara's gaze turns fierce. I see a fleeting image of the warriors of her past cross her features.

"Oh? Is that all?" I say. "Take whatever land in the vineyard you like. There's plenty of room."

The smile she wears slips. When it comes back, it's clearly forced. "You don't understand how ownership works, do you?"

"My mother sold me to a demon when I was just a boy." I shrug; the words tumble from my mouth easily for the facts that they are. "I was born a slave. I've always been someone's property."

Her forced smile falls under the weight of my words. The

17

sharp end of the blade she's holding points down. Zahara looks at me, horror-struck.

"Oh, I don't blame her. It wasn't as though she loved me. Maternal love is a fairly new human concept. Most animals pop out their offspring and leave them to fend for themselves. My mother did feed and clothe me for a few years, at least."

Zahara only stares at me. She doesn't smile. I don't know the words to say to bring back that grin. It seems inappropriate to bring up my dick and her vagina after talking about my mother.

I'm not sure. I wish Gaius was here to advise me. Though he was born lowly like me, his manners are perfect. I never bothered with the niceties of table manners and polite speech. No one ever wanted anything from me north of my cock.

What I do like is having Zahara's attention fully focused on me. Her dark gaze roams with a bright light of compassion. But then she blinks, as though catching herself. She closes her eyes and looks away.

"Are you hurt?" I reach out to her.

She moves back. The pointy end of the blade is pointed once again at my heart. Doesn't she know it's her frown that cuts me more than that edge ever could?

"You're trying to get in my head, aren't you? Trying to make me feel sympathy for you so that I'll let you go."

"Do you mean mind control?"

The fact that she's now glaring at my ear instead of directly into my eyes tells me the answer.

"I don't have that talent," I assure her. "Compelling takes a lot of focus. My mind wanders a lot. I was likely dropped on my head as a baby."

Her glare leaves my ear and returns to my eyes. I wish I

could hold her there. Having her eyes on mine makes me feel clearheaded for the first time in my life.

"I can hardly look at myself in the mirror," I say. "But I can't seem to take my eyes off you."

The corner of Zahara's right eye twitches, as though she's trying to determine whether to believe me or not. I hold still for her examination. I've never been to school or had any formal learning, other than Hadrian insisting I learn my letters. Whatever test Zahara gives me now, I am determined to pass.

"I don't lie. Not with my words, anyway." I look down at the growing bulge in my pants.

Zahara's gaze dips too. "Looks like your body knows what it wants."

I shake my head. "Both me and my dick desire you. But like I said, I won't let it hurt you."

"You talk about your penis as though it's not a part of you."

"It has a mind of its own. Believe me when I tell you it's too big for you. Would you like to see for yourself?"

I reach for my zipper and peel it down. As I do so, the blade falls from Zahara's hand and she gasps. With feline grace, she springs from the bed and lands on the floor as the monster makes its appearance from between the teeth of my zipper.

CHAPTER 4

ZAHARA

I've spent most of my life living in Central America. In that land of lush green forests and wetlands, there are many large animals that can kill you, one of them being the Anaconda. I've seen my fair share of the large snakes slithering around, looking for a meal. None of those beasts could hold a twig to the massive tree trunk that Virius Serrano takes out of his pants.

I leap back, away from him and to the door. The hackles of the big cat in me rise, now on high alert as I sense a threat.

I hiss at the sight of the predator as it slithers towards me. There is no tongue that slithers out of its mouth. Only a single bead of moisture that leaks from its solitary eye. I swear that eye tracks me as more of the beast's body slithers from its hiding space between Virius's thighs.

Is he carrying that thing around with him the whole time? How does he stay upright? How has it not attacked him? If it gets close enough, it will certainly swallow me whole—from the tip of my head on down to my pinky toes.

Virius's cock is thick enough to take me whole. He's definitely long enough to have his fill of me. And that thing is supposed to go inside me?

I sincerely don't see that happening. It defies the laws of biology. It defies the laws of physics.

"It won't hurt you," Virius says as he holds the massive beast out towards me. He can barely contain his cock in his hands, and his hands are nearly the size of my head.

The pulsing of that one-eyed monster begs to differ with his words. It throbs as it looks at me. The red tip grows darker with each second as blood pools there. The veins at the sides of the python's length also coil and writhe as he grows longer. Thicker. Closer. Readying to eat me alive.

So why do I want to reach out and touch it? Why do I have the urge to pet it and give it a name? Peter the Python. Anthony the Anaconda. Lenard the Lady Killer. Frankie the Fucking Big Dick Monster.

"Now you see why I won't have sex with you," Virius says.

He shoves his dick back into his pants. It's a two hand job. The large, reddened flesh definitely fights him as he wrestles it back below his waistband.

It does not go. He heaves a sigh of frustration as he gives up the battle with his zipper. Instead of continuing the wrestling bout, Virius yanks the threadbare sheet over his waist.

I can still see the clear outline beneath the cloth. Frankie pulses with life. Still writhing, coiling, and pulsing. I would swear it's trying to get closer to me.

Anacondas aren't as dangerous as Hollywood movies and documentaries make them out to be. Snakes, large or small, aren't aggressive creatures. They generally go out of their way to avoid large animals, especially humans. If they attack, it's because they feel threatened. Or they're hungry.

The thing in Virius's pants continues to move, tenting the sheets, as he stretches his hands behind his head and grins up at me.

"You are small and tiny, just a wee thing. Your cunny would split in two if the beast got too close."

Said cunny pulses and clenches as I continue to stare at his covered midsection. Then my mind replays his words and my lady bits' desires get pushed to the back of my thoughts. "Did you just call me small? Tiny? And wee?"

I straighten from my crouch to my full height. So maybe I'm nowhere near the six and a half feet of Virius's height. I'm barely at his eye level as he lounges back on the cot.

Taking a few steps toward him, I retrieve my dagger. I flip it in my palm, catching the handle and aiming the pointy end at him. Virius grins at my show of violence.

"And fierce." He grins down at the dagger in my hand. "You would gut me if I let you."

If he let me? Does he not see who has the upper hand here? Clearly, in my upper hand is a blade that I just demonstrated I know how to use. Like I said, he isn't the first Anaconda I've ever seen.

"You are a treasure," Virius says.

That rankles. I've been told all my life that I am special. That my womb is sacred. Its purpose is to free my people and bring us wealth and happiness. And for that belief, I—along with my magical, virgin vagina—am a treasure.

But at the way Virius says the word *treasure*, I don't feel burdened by another's desires of me. His gaze asks nothing of me. He looks at me with delight. With amusement. Like he wants to play with me.

The boys I grew up with never wanted to play with me.

The girls, either. Treasures are coveted, looked at, not handled in fun.

The blade in my hold falters at my thought of having a little enjoyment. Not out of duty or a sacred rite—which by the way were never any laughs. I've never enjoyed blowing off steam for no good reason.

"What can I do to please you?"

I blink my eyes a few times to bring Virius back into focus. My mind must have drifted. Did he just ask me what I want?

"I'm not giving you my cock." He ticks off that item with his thumb, and said thumb is just as blunt as said cock. His long index finger joins his thumb as he continues his list. "You don't want me to give you my land. Tell me what I can do to bring you pleasure."

His words make no sense. It has to be some kind of trick. He's trying to make a ploy to escape. "You're trapped. You know that, right?"

Virius looks around the cave he walked into last night as though seeing it for the first time. The rocky walls are a smooth, slate gray. The cot and threadbare sheets are the only furnishings in the room. Behind me is a locked door that opens from the outside.

"Do you wish me to stay?" he asks.

"You kinda have no choice. Trapped, remember?"

Virius nods as though turning my words over in his head. Decision apparently made, he nods. "Then I'll stay."

I give my head a shake. I'd heard he isn't playing with a full deck up there. But now I see that the rumors are true. This man might be crazy.

"Would you like me to pet you?" Virius says. "Cats like to be scratched behind their ears and on their bellies."

One: I'm not some house cat. I'm a jaguar—a panther, actually, because my coat is midnight black and I have no spots. Two: he must not have come into contact with any kind of domestic cat before because not a single feline would let a hand anywhere near its belly without sinking in claws or teeth.

"Or having your tail stroked. Would you like me to do that?"

"No, I—ah."

With cat-like reflexes, Virius snakes his hand out and grabs me. My hand opens in protest. When it does, my knife clatters to the floor.

I'm not defenseless. I've been trained to take down assailants. Though I don't feel under attack by his hands.

Virius brings me to him, picking me up as though I weigh nothing and sitting me on his lap like I am some damn house cat. His lap is still covered by the sheet, but it's not much of a barrier for what he's packing. Before I can yowl in protest, his hands are on me.

To my utter shock and embarrassment, I let out a low purr as his long, thick fingers find a spot behind my ear and he rubs me there. Somehow, he knows the right pressure.

His fingers have me shuddering, mewling as he hits the right spots. I am ready to curl into him and rub myself against him. I am knife-less, defenseless, and ready to show him my belly as long as he keeps scratching at that particular itch that I never knew I had.

CHAPTER 5

VIRIUS

*Z*ahara trembles at my touch. My little cat is a small, wee thing. Whereas I am a monster, a blunt object used to smash and stuff into small things that like to be broken.

For a moment, fear grips me hard. Have I hurt her? It's always been difficult for me to tell the difference between pleasure and pain. Women's cries of passion as their flesh bleeds from my pounding sound the same as a prisoners' screams as I ripped off their fingernails.

I know my strength. What I don't know is how to be gentle with all the power I wield in this overlarge body of mine. Tenderness has never once been requested of me.

Not when I fought for every scrap on the streets of ancient Rome. Not when I whored for Domitia. Not when I was an executioner for Inquisitors.

My little cat purrs as she shudders. That is a good sign. That is a sign of pleasure.

Animals, I have always understood. The sounds they make to showcase their intentions are clear. A low growl as a warning. A high-pitched rumble as an invitation.

Zahara's sigh rolls off her tongue. The sound, beginning from high in her nasal cavity, reminds me of the coiffed singers in the theater that Gaius liked. Those women always sounded to me as though they were screaming along with the music. The sound that comes from Zahara is like that, but pleasant to my ears.

As my fingers continue to stroke her, she hits a higher note. And then an even higher one. Her eyes are closed, but I still see her lashes flutter. Another sign of pleasure. My chest puffs out at the thought that I have brought her this satisfaction.

I run my nails behind her ears. Her lobes are shaped like teardrops, reminding me of individual grapes hanging from the vine. I let my fingers follow the curve of her ear.

She shudders again. Her small breasts rub against my shirt. I have the urge to rip away the fabric between us and feel her flesh against mine. I look at the handfuls on her chest. What would it be like to cup them in my hands? What would it be like to taste them with my tongue?

I banish the thought before it can take more shape. Women have only ever wanted me to squeeze their breasts until they reddened. To punish their nipples with a vice formed by my blunt fingers until they screamed from an orgasm. Even if Zahara wanted that treatment, I don't think I could give it to her. Seeing even the slightest red mark from my hand on her dark skin would gut me.

Gentleness is still a new thing for me. It's a skill I'll need to master before allowing any more contact than this. I'll need to ask Gaius for guidance. He is a master of women's pleasure. Giving it. Withholding it. Prolonging it.

Hadrian, on the other hand, likes to tie up his vampire wife, Carignan. But from her screams, which are filled with declarations of love for him, I gather she likes it.

I don't want to hold Zahara down. I know what it is like to be bound and forced against your will until you have no will left. No, I want her to seek me out for pleasure. Just like a cat would curl up in its master's lap.

Just as she's doing now as I stroke her.

The sound of her purring makes the beast grow harder. It throbs and pulses, eager to get at her. The head of my cock rubs away at the thin sheet separating us. It's blunt but it could punch a hole in the cotton with the right amount of friction.

I need to put it away. To jam it back inside my pants, which are now too small. Though I know it's a fool's errand. The monster has reared its head. It won't go down without a fight. I don't have much fight in me with heaven in my arms.

Zahara is pressing her face into the palm of my hand. She rubs her cheek against my fingers, as though she's seeking more of my touch. The sensation is so foreign to me that I stop petting to watch her now pet me.

From a distance, the angles of her heart-shaped face had appeared sharp. Now that I'm holding her cheekbones, I feel the softness of the flesh there. There are fine hairs along her temples that tickle my fingertips. I stare at them in wonder as her softness, her heat, her nearness, invade all of my senses.

Does she realize that I am now wrapped around her little finger? Does she understand that my entire world view has narrowed down to encompass only her? Does she know that I have her scent, and will follow her wherever she goes until the end of time?

She says she's trapped me. She is entirely right. My cage is here inside the palm of her hand, and I will never leave willingly. If she wants to keep me underground in this room, in this bed, I will gladly stay.

I am so hyper-aware of all the new sensations that I miss the invasion. An unfamiliar sensation presses against my mouth. It's Zahara. She rubs her lips against mine—once, twice. And then she presses forward. I jerk away from her before she can...

I'm not sure what she had planned.

Zahara's eyes slam open. She gulps and looks around as though she's forgotten where she is. Her brown cheeks are stained red. But it's a darker shade of red than passion. She looks embarrassed.

"What did you just do?" I ask her.

"Me? I didn't do anything. You're the one who got all handsy."

She swats at my hands. I do not loosen my hold on her, though I am mindful of my strength. I only exert enough power to keep her in my lap, pressed against my chest so that she cannot escape.

"With your mouth?" I say. "What was that?"

"Don't get all excited that I kissed you. It didn't mean anything. I was just sampling the milk, since I've already bought the cow."

Zahara continues to push and shove at my chest. She turns her head away, avoiding my questioning gaze.

"That was a kiss?"

Her face reddens. She manages to get an elbow free and uses it to deliver an uppercut. I merely grunt and tighten my hold. She is strong for a little thing. But she doesn't realize she is mine and I will not let her go.

"No one's ever done that to me before," I say.

Zahara stops struggling. She turns back to me, her lips parted in a perfect O.

I gaze at the shape. My eyes do a full circuit of her upper and lower lips, remembering their softness. I knew what a kiss was, though it was rare to see in a whorehouse. Patrons came to have their loins plundered, not their lips.

"Do it again," I say. Then, remembering my manners, I add, "Please."

Zahara's breathing is heavy. But she's stopped struggling. Something else that has stopped throbbing is the beast below. It appears just as entranced by the kiss as the rest of me.

I taste the sweetness of her breath as she exhales once more. My tongue aches to trace her lips. My belly aches to drink her down. Not her blood—though I wouldn't mind a taste of that, as well. But right now, I just want her. Her breath mixed with mine. Her essence inside of me.

Barely a couple of inches separate us. Zahara's lips are right there for the taking. I hunger for her mouth, but I don't want to do it wrong.

"Show me how?" I say. And then I remember, belatedly, "Please."

She swallows, and I want to growl in protest. I wanted to taste that.

One of my hands releases the hold I have on her face. My fingers slide down her body to rest on her hip, to hold her steady and not let her go.

"Please," I repeat. It's the last time I'll ask. Then I'm going to take.

"Sure," she says. Though she fails at the nonchalance I think she's aiming for. "Why not? We'll be fucking soon anyway."

I don't correct her. I was being truthful when I said I wouldn't have sex with her. Down below, the monster in my pants calls me a liar. He's only patient now because he wants to taste her as much as the rest of me does.

Zahara leans in. I try to wait, to be patient, to follow her lead. But then, like the brute I was raised to be, I strike.

CHAPTER 6

ZAHARA

*T*he man is lying. He has to be lying. I'm not buying that a four-hundred-year-old vampire has not kissed a woman in all his unnatural life. But I don't care if it is all a lie, a bit of a Roman-tic game to loosen me up, because hell, can the lying fiend kiss.

He made it seem like he didn't know what he was doing when I first brushed my lips to his. Now that he is brushing his lips against mine, it is clear he knows exactly what he wants. And what he wants is me.

If I hadn't known that from Frankie still stirring beneath me, like lightning was striking volts into his balls, then I would know it by the way Virius growled low and deep in the back of his throat at the second brush of our lips.

At first, I was the only one out in the storm. Now, Virius is with me every step of the way. Using his lower lip, he tests the touch of my top lip. Moving his head back and forth in a slow, sensuous motion, he covers every part of my mouth, from the corner, to the seam, to the divot at the center.

I feel devoured by this man, and he isn't even using any tongue. Not that I've had anyone tongue kiss me before. Unless he's lying to me, this is the first kiss for both of us.

The more Virius's mouth moves against mine, the more I begin to believe him. Not because of his inexperience. Because of how he revels in the experience.

It's the same way that I am getting caught up in the unfamiliar contact. We both take our time exploring. There is no rush to get to a particular part because it's all new territory. From the way he pulls me closer with each stroke, and the way I come to him without protest, I gather we both are thoroughly enjoying this brave new world.

The moment Virius's tongue sneaks from his mouth and into mine, I lose control. His licks are not tentative flicks. He's a man trying a new dessert, as though he knows he will clean the plate and order a second serving.

He licks at me in long, silky strokes. Then his tongue disappears into his mouth to savor what he's captured. After another of those low growls, he licks again. And then again.

Virius bites at my bottom lip, tentatively, as though he thinks he might hurt me. I should be worried that he'll bite me. That is his natural instinct. But he only nibbles softly, as though I am an appetizer. When my lips part, he starts in on the main course.

He licks into my mouth like I am a rare steak. His tongue sweeps over me, devouring me. I meet his tongue finally. The first flick of my tongue catches the sharp side of one of his fangs.

I feel the tiny pinprick like a needle. Then there's the metallic taste of blood. Virius's tongue circles around mine. He snatches the droplet away and then sucks. Hard.

I should be afraid. A vampire has tasted my blood. But the

feel of him pulling from me, the knowledge that he is swallowing a piece of me down, it turns me all the way on.

I squirm in his lap, needing to feel the same kind of friction between my thighs. Frankie coils beneath me, ready and eager to slither his way into my depths.

Virius's hold on me tightens. His hands lock me down so I can't wriggle away. Not that I'm trying to escape.

The anaconda between his thighs slithers higher and throbs at my core. It pokes at the bud at the apex of my thighs. Like Eve, I want the snake to take a bite.

Somewhere in the room, a throat clears behind us. I wonder if it's the voice of God. Is he looking down from on high and showing his displeasure at the sin about to go down beneath the garden on the surface?

I don't have the chance to look up to see if it's the Heavenly Father. I'm being thrown onto the bed. Virius puts himself between me and the throat-clearer. His large body blocks me from seeing who has come into the locked room. The menace that runs off him should scare me, but it turns me on.

I've had men protect me before. But each one had done it for his own gain. I know without a doubt that Virius is sticking his neck out for me because he wants to please me.

If I were a weaker woman, I'd reach up and twirl my hair. I'd swoon back on the bed and let him fight this battle for me. Unfortunately, that's not the woman I was raised to be. That level of inaction isn't how I was taught to move through the world.

I look over to see Itzel standing in the doorway. My aunt is no match for this vampire. But like the fierce warrior she is, she holds her ground, teeth bared and dagger in hand.

When I try to move around Virius, he puts out a meaty paw, holding me back. Does he still not realize who is the captor and who is the captive here?

"Down, boy," I say. I get off the cot and move around him. "This is Itzel."

"She's your kin?" asks Virius.

Technically, she's not my blood. Both my parents are dead. I have no direct relatives left. But I do claim the women of this tribe as my family. So, I nod to Virius.

And just like that, the menace rolls away from his large body. His entire being changes from one of destruction to a teddy bear—a soft grizzly of a teddy bear with sharp claws and deadly fangs.

I want to cuddle into him.

I am so fucked in the head.

"My apologies," he says. "That's probably not the impression I should make if I want to impress your family."

Itzel isn't looking at his face. Her gaze is below his belt, because he isn't wearing a belt, and he never refastened his pants. They are down around his ankles. Frankie stands as erect as a flag pole. His one eye salutes Itzel.

The older woman clears her throat before she jerks her gaze away. "You're needed, Zahara."

It takes me a moment to tear my gaze away from Frankie. The little monster certainly knows how to get attention. I walk to the door.

When Virius starts to follow, pants still around his ankles, I hold up my hand. "No, you stay here."

He frowns at me.

"You're my captive, remember?"

The frown doesn't leave his handsome face. Nor does he make a move to pull up his pants.

"Go back to the bed, or I'll have to bring out the chains."

"You like bondage?"

I realize he's asking a legitimate question. Not a hint of kink-shaming.

"I'll be back later," I say, avoiding his question and, more importantly, avoiding my piqued interest in the subject matter.

Virius bends, giving me a delectable view of his ass. It's just as nice as the front package. When he straightens, I see that he has a dagger pointed at me. My dagger.

"Here," he says, handing it to me.

I want to tell him that no one here will hurt me. Instead, I say nothing. I'm gratified that Itzel didn't see that I had dropped not only my guard against my prisoner, but also my weapon.

Virius toes off his pants, then he kicks them into a corner of the cave. With one final glance over my shoulder, I see him go and sit on the bed, lounging as a panther would. I tear my gaze from him and follow Itzel down the narrow passageway.

"What do you think you're doing, playing with that demon like that?" she demands once we are out of the vampire's earshot. "Remember your role, Zahara. Remember your purpose."

As if I could forget. It's been drilled into my head since before I could form words. As I open my mouth to speak, I see shadows moving from the wall, some in feline form, others on human legs. They all converge on me, gazes flashing, shining the bright light of sacred responsibility directly into my eyes.

"I know," I say. "My womb will birth the child to save our land and our kind."

"Don't forget the other part," says Itzel. "The prophecy says he'll die before the child is born. So don't get attached."

CHAPTER 7

VIRIUS

I can't keep my fingers off my lips. They still tingle from where I pressed them to Zahara's. They feel swollen, like I've been punched in the mouth. I've been hit in the face many times; the majority of blows came when I was still human.

If it wasn't my mother, or the *lena*, or one of the *puellas* of the brothel knocking me out of their way, then it was someone on the street throwing into me. As a human, I had to fight for every breath I took, every scrap of food I stole, every tendril of warmth I could scrounge. By the time Domitia turned me, I'd given up the fight.

I was scrawny and helpless as a child. I grew overlarge and stout when I came into my manhood. As a vampire, I had the power to take whatever I wanted. But by then there was nothing that I craved.

It was what Gaius called irony. Something or other to do with opposites that are funny. I laugh now as I run my fingers over my swollen lips. It was a wee cat who had taken a swing at me and landed me on my ass.

I settle down on the uncomfortable cot. I slept on cobblestones as a boy. For centuries, I've had the luxury of feathers and down and memory foam beneath me. I don't want to get used to the rickets of this poor excuse for a bed. Tomorrow, I'll take Zahara back to the house and wrap her in silks.

Though, she is a cat. She might prefer feathers.

I lick my lips at the thought of her covered in feathers. The taste of her is still in the corner of my mouth. There's even a hint of her blood on my tongue.

She is O-positive; the most common blood type on the planet. On any other day, I would pass on that type. I always find it bitter and flat at the same time.

Not so when it comes from Zahara's veins. With just the drop of her lifeblood, I have a rush of sensation to my head. My teeth ache at the sweetness of it. My hunger grumbles for some more of it. I know from this moment on, from this taste, I will never drink anything else.

Zahara wants me to lie with her, to fuck her? Oh, irony is having its fun with me today. That will not happen. Though the beast below begs to differ, I will keep my monster cock from her.

I will be happy to kiss her senseless for the rest of her life. I will spend my nights scratching and petting her. Then I'll sip my fill from her lips. And later, when she allows it, I'll tap one of her veins for my sustenance.

I close my eyes to wait for her return. In the silence of the cave, I hear her voice. She's far away from the hovel she's left me in. But I sense her distress. She feels cornered, trapped.

My feet are on the floor before I have any conscious thought of moving. The closed and locked door isn't even a thought. When it meets the thrust of my shoulder, it learns it was never an obstacle. Not if it stands between me and her.

The voices are still faint, but they aren't my guide. Zahara's scent is. I can smell the agitation in it and that makes me move faster. I have to remind myself that she has a dagger. I saw her wield it the other day against males of her kind.

My little kitten can hold her own in a fight. It made my cock stir to watch her take the larger males down. And then she turned that dagger on me. My heart had never beaten so wildly in my life.

It thuds hard in my chest as I run to find her. The thuds ring in my ears because my blood supply is low. I haven't eaten for nearly two days. But my blood lust will have to wait until I make sure that Zahara is safe.

When I round a corner, I see her. She's surrounded. But not by male shifters. She's surrounded by women. All of them older. All of them with the smell of fur.

Zahara has her back to a corner as the women close in around her. Not a single fist is raised. Only voices. It looks like they're all in the middle of an argument.

"Why should she wait?" says a woman who could only be described as a cougar. Her face is wizened with age, but her body is as supple as a coed's. "She might as well fuck him now and be done with it."

"It has to be done on a full moon, in accordance with the prophecy," says Itzel, the woman who came to fetch Zahara earlier.

"This is biology," says the cougar, "not magic. She is fertile now."

The arguing continues from both sides of the alcove. The only one not joining in is Zahara. She looks away from the shouting, as though she isn't hearing any of it. The faraway look in her gaze reminds me of myself, of all the times I was chained to a wall or strapped down to a bed so that a rich, upper-class woman could use my body to fill Domitia's coin purse or garner a favor.

I never needed to be strapped down. The chain hasn't been made that could hold me. The binds were an illusion for the human women who purchased my service. The reason I didn't fight was a whole other game that my mistress liked to play.

Domitia was known for her power plays. She'd had me mindfucked ever since I was a child. I always bent to her will. She got off on seeing the physical manifestation of my compliance.

Is that why Zahara is standing there in the middle of this argument? Has she been mindfucked by one or all of these women? They're talking about a prophecy. Didn't she say something to me about a prophecy?

I take a step towards her, ready to bulldoze my way through all of them to get to her. That's when I feel the dagger at my throat.

I only barely stop myself from taking the head of the person who threatens my life. Any other time during the last two centuries, I might not have cared that my life might end. It had all been a misery. But tonight I have known happiness, and I want another taste of it. I want another taste of Zahara.

Therefore, I can't kill the woman behind me. She smells like Zahara. She must be kin. I don't think Zahara would like it if I decapitated her aunt or cousin.

"Go back the way you came," a feminine voice whispers into my ear. "Follow the passage and take the tunnel to the right. It will take you back to the surface."

"The surface?"

"You are trying to leave, aren't you? You are trying to escape?"

Why would I leave? This is where Zahara is. When I don't answer her immediately, she gives an irritated sigh.

"We'd heard you weren't right in the head."

That is what's whispered about me. It's likely true, though Gaius and Hadrian get pissed any time anyone dares to say it aloud. Which is why people never dare raise their voice above a whisper if they even dare to say it.

"You know what they're going to do to you?" the woman continues. "They're going to breed you. They're going to use your sperm to make a child. And then they'll—"

"Drop the knife, Pia."

I turn at the sound of Zahara's voice. She still has her back against the wall. But even from this distance, I can see the tension in her limbs. She's poised to pounce, like a jaguar scenting its prey.

Her gaze flashes a bright yellow. Her skin bristles, like it's not flesh, but fur. Her white teeth flash and I catch a bit of fang. It causes the beast below to stir with desire for her.

"He's trying to escape," says Pia.

And then there are more daggers, fangs, and fur. But when I look up, all I see is Zahara. There is a flash of hurt in her dark eyes before her features turn to steel.

CHAPTER 8

ZAHARA

"I just want to make sure you understand what's at stake here, child," Itzel says, bringing my attention back to the lecture at hand.

I had drifted off as the voices of the women rose up from both sides of me. Those standing on the right with Itzel are the purists. They believe that I should follow the letter of the prophecy and wait to give up the goods at the appointed time, which is the full moon in two nights' time.

Those prowling on the left are led by Zuma, who isn't a jaguar. She was originally from my father's tribe but moved down to Guatemala a generation ago. Though she is a cougar, the jaguar shifters accept her. What isn't so acceptable is her disregard for the old ways of the Maya.

"I just want to make sure she knows she can use his stake for a little fun before she has to get down to business," says Zuma, giving me a wink.

I don't return the cheeky gesture. I purse my lips and let

the air out through my nose. For all of my life, others have made decisions for me based on my destiny. I am supposed to birth a child to save our tribe. Yet even after I reached my maturity, everyone continued treating me like a child. If I mouthed off, I'd be treated as a child. If I held quiet, I'd be treated as a child.

I'd thought that when I got rid of the males, things would change. The women trust me, but I'm still the youngest of the group. And so I'm still treated as a child.

"It is her destiny to release us from the curse," says Itzel.

"I know," says Zuma. "But that doesn't mean she has to act like a sacrifice."

Oh, the irony. The women in our history were given as sacrifices to gods. But they also ruled. There were times of harmony before colonialism brought in the patriarchy and destroyed our matrilineal history.

I tune them out again and let them lecture on. I've only ever wanted a lecture from an actual college professor. I want to sit in a lecture hall on an uncomfortable hardback chair and scribble down notes with different colored pens. But nope. I'm going to be changing the diapers of a supernatural baby instead.

I know there are thousands of women who go to school and raise a family at the same time. I even pointed out that I will have a literal village of women to help me raise my child. But that didn't sway them either. I'll still be barefoot and pregnant.

Well, not barefoot. Zuma did gift me with a nice pair of heels last month. Not that I'll get to wear them anywhere except, maybe, the delivery room.

Thoughts of the delivery room take me back to how this child will be made. With a man trapped in a room not too far from where I'm standing. I press my lips together, seeking any hint of Virius's taste on my mouth.

He's there. Just at the center of my lower lip. I tug the flesh I find there into my mouth and pull at the skin.

There is a note of the sweetness of the ripest grape. The robust smoke of wood. And a hint of iron, but there's no metallic taste.

Out of the corner of my eye, I see a vision of him. He's standing in that ridiculous shirt featuring a caricature of my culture. The jeans are off, but the chaps still hang around his thick thighs. Peeking out from the leather of the chaps is Frankie. He raises his head as though he's looking for me. That single eye finds me, and a dollop of precum beads at the tip, as though Virius's dick is salivating.

Damn, I'm hard up. I should probably take Zuma's advice and jump Virius tonight—if I can get him to let me ride him. He'll probably be more amenable now that Pia has a dagger at his throat.

Wait.

What?

I blink. Then I blink again. I'm not fantasizing.

Virius stands on the other side of the cave. Pia is behind him with a dagger at his throat. A bead of his blood trickles down his thick neck.

"Drop the knife, Pia." I'm moving as I talk, but I falter at Pia's next words.

"He's trying to escape."

My brain is beyond considering how Virius escaped the locked room. It focuses only on the one word: escape. He was trying to leave? He said he wouldn't. He said he'd stay.

Maybe I should let him go. If he's not here, then he can't impregnate me. If I'm not pregnant, then maybe I can go to college. And if he doesn't fulfill the prophecy, then he can't fulfill the part where he dies.

I give the voice in my head a rough shake. Neither of us can escape this prophecy. Destiny always finds you.

43

It doesn't matter what he wants, just as it doesn't matter what I want. Virius is going back under lock and key, and we are getting it on. He's going to put a baby in me whether he likes it or not.

All around me I hear feminine gasps. For a second, I worry that I've said that out loud. But I quickly realize that not a single eye, human or jaguar, is on me. Every female in this room is looking at the monster swaying between Virius's thighs.

Frankie is lifted high, with no hand from Virius. That cheeky snake leans a little to the right, and then to the left, as though he's dancing to an unheard snake charmer's tune. Then I realize Frankie is swaying in time to my beat as I march towards him and Virius.

"I wasn't going anywhere," he says when I reach him. "I thought I heard you in distress."

Once again, I'm brought up short. The man is my captive, and he thought he was coming to save me? He has a real hero complex.

"Now I see why she might want to anticipate the full moon."

I'm not sure I know who said it. But I know they all are thinking it now that they see what Virius is working with.

"Are all vampires hung like that?"

"I don't know, but I want to find out."

I slap Pia's hand away from Virius's neck. I glare at her, flashing my eyes. She's older than I am—all of them are. But she bows her head in deference.

Unlike wolves, jaguars don't have a hierarchal order. They are mostly loners. The only time they spend together as a pack is when they're raising cubs. Otherwise, they're highly territorial.

Pia's lucky I only slapped her hand and didn't bite it off. I take Virius by the upper arm and turn him so all the others can see of him is his ass. I only barely hold myself back from dropping trow and peeing on his leg. Only barely.

Now that they've all seen who he belongs to, I give him a tug to leave. Virius is larger and stronger than me. I know I would have no pull over him if he didn't want to go with me. Luckily, he follows my lead and we head back to the bedroom.

He doesn't know he's following me to his doom. I tell myself I don't care. He is not my destiny. The child is. He is only a tool, and I plan to use him.

CHAPTER 9

VIRIUS

We walk in silence down the stony pathway. My bare feet slap against smooth rocks. Her boots crunch along, grinding small stones into sand.

There is an itch at the center of my palm. I want to reach out and take her slight paw into mine like I've seen Hadrian do with Cari. I've never held a woman's hand before. What if I do it wrong? What if I crush her slender fingers in mine?

Looking down at her hand, I see that her fingers are not so slender. Her nails are short, not long and painted like Marechal's. Zahara's worked in the Durand vineyard for years. She knows the roughness of turning soil. She knows the prick of pruning shears. She undoubtedly can't handle my cock, but perhaps she can handle my hand.

Without a second thought, I reach for her.

"Ouch." I grimace, pulling my hand back from hers.

A trail of crimson beads at the tip of my forefinger. It's blood I can't afford to lose. Pressing my finger to my mouth,

I look back down at Zahara's hand. How had I missed the gleam of the blade there?

"Were you trying to disarm me?" she asks.

"I was trying to hold your hand."

Zahara looks down at her hand; her fingers tighten on the hilt of her dagger. There isn't suspicion in her gaze, only confusion. As though she questions my battle tactic.

"Why?" she says.

I shrug, too embarrassed to explain. I might be Roman, but I am clearly not cut out for these antics. I need to dispense with the attempts at romance from here on out.

We have come to the end of the hall and can go no further. The mangled door blocks our path. Bending down, I pick it up as though the metal slab weighs nothing, because it doesn't for me. I turn and wait for Zahara to go inside.

She doesn't move. She stands there, staring at the door, then at me. "You weren't trying to escape?"

There's something in her voice. It's not fear; I know what that smells like. It's acrid on my tongue, bitter like hopelessness. But I can't be sure. I've long since forgotten both of those emotions. I've had so few feelings for most of my life. My default setting is numb and detached.

This night with her, I am drowning in awareness and sensation. I don't care to come up for air if Zahara is the flood. I'm more than happy to exist as a piece of driftwood in the ocean of her.

"I told you I'd stay," I say.

She narrows her eyes as she looks from me to the door in my hands.

"I heard raised voices. I thought you were in trouble," I add.

Zahara rolls her eyes at that. Her shoulders slump, like a child who's just had a reprimand. She walks into the room

47

and plops down on the cot. "Close the door behind you, will you?" she says.

I do as she bids me, fitting the door back into place. The knob will no longer work, which means the lock won't engage. I doubt any of the shifters have the strength to remove the slab. So, we will have our privacy.

Once I'm certain that we are isolated, I turn to her. Her gaze isn't on my face. It dips to my waist. She's looking down at the beast.

I bend down and gather my jeans from the floor. I don't bother to step either leg into the pants. Clearly, I'll lose the battle of wrangling my cock into the cloth. Stepping out of the chaps, I then tear the fabric of the leather With a quick tie, I have a makeshift toga. My native garb is far more comfortable than the fashion of the day. Gaius always acts as though he's got a pebble in his Italian loafers when I deign to walk around in this fashion.

Zahara doesn't complain. Which reminds me of something.

"Why were you arguing?" I ask as I finish making the knot to hold the fabric and the beast in place.

"Because of the prophecy. I told them you don't want to fuck me. Even though we both know that isn't true."

Her gaze is on my crotch. Though I've tied the beast up, it remains staunchly erect. Its fat head points directly at Zahara, as though asking her for a dance.

"That can't be comfortable," she says.

It's not. My balls are starting to turn blue, since the monster has been erect for the better part of a couple of hours.

"My sire used cock rings to keep her new bucks in order. If they displeased her, she'd yank out a valve of their hearts and lecture them as the wound healed. Or cut off their testicles if they fucked another without her permission."

Zahara gasps. Her gaze finally leaves my groin area and comes to my face.

"Oh, those grow back," I assure her. "There's a vampire queen in Africa who makes eunuchs out of her human warriors. I hear that makes them obedient."

Domitia might have played with the testes but she never whacked off the penises of her sireds. I've always thought it would be better to be a eunuch. But my cock would grow back. I know that for a fact as well.

"You weren't trying to escape," Zahara says. It's not a question this time.

"I'll never leave you," I say as I settle down on the cot beside her. "You're mine."

"You do remember that I captured you."

"That you did." I grin. "And I'm yours."

"Then you're going to have to fuck me and put a baby in me. Why don't we just get it over with now?"

She begins to unbutton her shirt. I don't stop her. I want to see her breasts.

The twin peaks that appear as she parts her shirt do not disappoint. They are lush brown mounds, topped with the darkest chocolate tips. My mouth waters and my fangs sharpen.

"Can I kiss them?"

Zahara grins, like a cat who has the cream within reach of her paws. She nods, and then gasps as I descend upon her.

I first take the left one in my mouth. I moan at the unexpected taste I find there. I expected her to be nothing but sweetness. Instead, her nipple is the rich bite of dark chocolate. The taste is harsh and not for the faint of heart, just like my wee warrior. The cocoa nibs are tart. They fill me with the warmth of a roasted flame.

I gather her body to me. My panther doesn't fight me. She

49

wraps her arms around my back and digs her fingers into my hair. I feel claws. And I like it.

Her moan turns to a yelp as I flip her over onto her back. Then I'm on top of her, tonguing every lick of salt I find from the undersides of her breasts, in the valley between the two, and into the nooks and crannies of her pebbled nipples.

"Please, Virius, inside me."

Zahara lets go of my hair and reaches for my cock. Before she can work her fingers into the knot of my toga, I snag both her wrists in mine. She fights me, yanking to break free of my hold. She's strong, but I'm stronger. My fear of hurting her lessens.

"You want me inside you?" I ask.

"Finally, he's getting it," she huffs.

I keep my hold on her wrists with my left hand. I bring the fingers of my right hand between us. "Open."

Zahara opens her thighs. I grin down at her. The cheeky kitten. Instead of clarifying my meaning, I bring my mouth to hers. When my lips meet hers, she obeys my original command.

I get lost in the kiss. Lost in her. In the taste, the touch, and feel of her. Her breasts were a dark treat, but her mouth is silky sweet. I'm so lost in the tangle of our tongues that I forget my original purpose.

Oh, right. She wanted me inside her. I'm going to oblige her.

With reluctance, I disentangle my tongue from hers. But I leave her mouth with one last, long lick. It causes Zahara to leave her mouth open, waiting for more. I take the opportunity to dip my index finger between her lips.

She suckles on the digit. The suction causes my cock to steal even more of the low blood supply in my system. I nearly lose my head as Zahara swirls her tongue around my finger, mimicking what she might do to my cock. But like I said, that will never happen. She is far too wee to take on that monster.

With my finger wet, I pull it from her mouth. Zahara whimpers in protest. But when she realizes where my hand is going, she moans with delight.

I slip my finger beneath the waistband of her cargo pants. There isn't a second waistband that I need to pass beneath her pants. She's not wearing any panties.

My finger takes its time trekking through the soft curls that hide her treasure. This is not a treasure hunt. I know exactly where the X of her spot is. I simply want to explore her body for a few seconds longer.

It's not just her body I want to explore. It's the feelings coming to life inside of me. I've never wanted this with a woman before. Sex has always been a job, a means to an end. For the first time in my life, I feel anticipation. I feel desire.

"Please, Virius."

No woman has ever begged me before. If she was a paying customer, she had free range to do with my body as she pleased. Zahara's plea breaks a dam inside me. I want to hear that cry again.

I find her clitoris. The little bud is so engorged that my finger slips off and to the side. Zahara gasps and bucks beneath me.

I rub her again, with the same effect. My index finger slips to the other side. I play slip and slide for a few moments, reveling in Zahara's cries. Marveling as I watch her body tremble at only my touch.

"Please, Viri, please."

She bucks and whimpers as I leave her clit. It's a short journey to her opening. I slip my finger inside her.

Well, I attempt to slip inside, but it's a tight fit.

Zahara's body tenses as the tip of my index finger breeches her virgin entrance. Immediately, I try to pull out of her untried flesh. Her body clamps down on my finger. She closes her legs, trapping me inside of her.

I don't complain. I work with what I'm given.

I move in and out of her. Just the tip of my finger. Just an inch, in and out.

"More, Viri, please."

I know that I shouldn't. But I can't deny her *please*.

Using my thumb, I gather the liquid desire that has pooled between her thighs. With my thumb lubricated, I return to her clit, which has swollen to twice the size since my index finger left it. I press her button with my thumb, making tiny circles.

It does the trick. Zahara's legs relax open. Her inner muscles give, letting my index finger slide into her. I'm up to the knuckle now.

"Ahh," she hisses.

The sound is a mix of pleasure and pain. With any other woman, I wouldn't be able to hear the difference. With any other woman, I wouldn't have cared.

When I look into Zahara's eyes, I see the pain is already melting away. All that remains is desire.

"Kiss me," she says.

I do as she asks. I give her what she wants. Because I am astounded that what she wants is me. My lips pressed against hers. My finger inside her.

Down below, the beast paces. It pulsates with a hunger that only grows. But I am prepared to starve that motherfucker. She can't handle my index finger. There's no way she can handle that fat prick.

I work my finger all the way inside her. At the same time, I rub her clit with my thumb. My lips capture her cries as she begins to tumble into ecstasy.

Zahara purrs against my lips as she climaxes, her body shaking and shivering. I swear I can see sparks from her skin as she shudders in ecstasy. There's a flash of obsidian fur as the tremors abate. Then she lies still.

Her eyes are closed. Her breathing is even. There's a satisfied smile on her face. She curls into my arms, just like a well-fed kitten, and falls asleep.

I pull my hand from her pants. The tip of my index finger is coated with her virgin's blood. I stare at the drop of crimson for a long moment. Then, with reverence, I place my finger in my mouth and suck.

My eyes close as more sparks fly behind my eyelids. She tastes like magic. She tastes like mine.

Below, the beast settles, secure in the knowledge that it will have its turn in due course. I push that thought away and pull Zahara securely into my arms. Then, for the first time in my life, I cuddle another living being.

CHAPTER 10

ZAHARA

J'm used to sleeping with other people. My family grew up poor, living in the poorest parts of towns and villages. There were always other cousins kicking out on the mattress and stealing the threadbare covers. I learned to train my mind to think of others' snores as night sounds from one of those fancy spa machines. The snorts and snuffles were accompanied by the chatter of the creepy crawlies out in the fields—which usually harmonized with the snores —because an open window was the only ventilation.

I wake to nothing but a hum in the underground cave. Virius doesn't snore. He is silent and still in his sleep, which is the reason why I woke. I've never had my own room, and I've never slept under the blanket of a man.

Virius is warm against my flesh. He doesn't kick or smother me. He holds me close to his chest, as though I am precious. His body is hunched to the edge of the cot in an uncomfortable position. He holds himself awkwardly, but he doesn't fidget. The vast majority of the small cot is left for me.

When I awoke, I worried that he might be dead. Because of the prophecy. Not because I care about him.

True, he just gave me an out of body experience with his fingers. Calling that orgasm an out of body experience is a big deal for a woman who can shift her body into another form. I'd nearly shifted as I shuddered in the onslaught of bliss. The panther in me had sat up and clawed to get out. She wanted to experience the pleasure first hand. She'd nearly gotten out, and would have if I hadn't fallen into the deepest, most contented sleep of my life.

All at the hands of this man. I shift to look down at him. He looks peaceful, boyish even. I tamp down that skip my heart just threatened.

Virius Serrano has no place in my heart. I have to fulfill my destiny, and he is the means to that end. Even though soon after, he will come to an end.

I move from under his arm. When I do, his hand flops down like a lifeless doll's. My heart skips that beat now. Maybe he is dead?

At the thought, my heart comes to a full stop. He can't be. He wasn't even inside me. There is no way I'm pregnant. The books I read weren't that graphic, but I know enough biology to know that a finger-fucking won't get me knocked up.

I cup my hand to Virius's cheek. He is cold to the touch. But I feel the slight hiss of breath from his nose. My chest loosens, and I begin to relax.

I have to remind myself: he is a vampire. He sleeps like the dead because he is not truly alive. He died hundreds of years ago.

I'm going to bang a quadricentenarian, yet the man doesn't look a day over twenty-one. That has to be how old he was when he was turned. So, technically, he's my age.

I brush a tendril of his curly hair from his face. He doesn't stir. For such a big and menacing-looking man, he is so soft.

Virius's features are relaxed in his sleep. Just looking at his face, it's hard to believe that he'd hurt a fly. If I'm honest, I can say that this man is beautifully created. At least my son will be handsome.

My fingers brush over Virius's broad shoulders. The span of them takes up the entire width of the small cot. My own body barely touches the mattress now. Virius is the cushion upon which my body rests. My torso is propped up on his chest and abs. My legs are twined with his.

I move my hand from his shoulders to the center of his chest. I'm surprised to find his heart beating. It's a faint beat but it's there. It's pumping someone else's blood through his system.

I wonder who he drank from last. I wonder if he'll be thirsty soon. The thought of him piercing my skin should be disgusting, but I press my thighs together as a vision of it flits through my mind.

I bend my leg at the knee and bump up against the anaconda in his toga. Virius is hard, erect, even in his sleep. I guess that beast never sleeps.

He says he won't have sex with me because he's so big and I'm so small. I'm sure every guy thinks that, but with Virius, it is one hundred percent true.

I saw what he is working with. It writhes beneath the cloth even now. His cock is the same thickness as my fore-arm, and just as long. He might be right. There is no way that thing is getting inside me comfortably.

So why does the thought of trying to fit it in arouse me?

I press my thighs together again. Belatedly, I forget that my knee is in his crotch. So instead of pressing my thighs together, I rub up against the anaconda. It slithers closer to me.

When Virius spoke about his dick, it wasn't with pride. It was with wariness. He spoke as though his manhood was separate from him as a man.

My hand trails down his chest, which is now bare and rid of that awful shirt. As I move south, the snake under wraps pulses against my thigh. With a glance upwards, I see that Virius still slumbers peacefully.

Maybe his dick does have a mind of its own because it is certainly not slumbering. It's coiling inside the fabric, like a snake being charmed by the movements of my hand. As I inch closer, it waves, bobbing and weaving to the sound of my quickening breaths.

I move closer. I am at the knot of the toga. With a tug of my thumb, the tie loosens. Just one more tug, and it'll be enough to set the monster free. The monster moves closer to the binding, ready to strike. My fingers poise to tug, and then—

A hand clamps down on my wrist. I look up to see Virius's eyes open and on me. He doesn't say a word, but censure is written all over his face.

"You know this is part of the deal," I say. "In two nights, there will be a lunar eclipse and we'll sleep together and make a baby; a son. It's prophesied."

"Prophecies are not always what they seem."

"It's my destiny to conceive your child and restore the rightful ownership and fruitfulness to the vineyard."

"I've given you the land." He kisses my fingertips, flicking his tongue over a hangnail I've been tugging at all day. "We are having trouble with the crop, but there are people working on it."

I know that Marechal Durand is working to figure out why the Serrano vines aren't bearing fruit. I tried to tell her her logic and chemicals would have no effect, but she didn't listen. Now she's mated to Gaius Serrano, which she doesn't seem at all put out about.

That still doesn't mean she can get the grapes to grow. Only breaking the curse will. And to do that, Virius will need to get busy putting a baby in me.

"I'm rich, you know," he says without any of the scumminess that a man born in wealth would say. "I can give you whatever you want."

"I want to fulfill my destiny. That means you coming inside me. Literally."

"You want me inside you, and you want to come?"

"Yes."

"Done."

Before I can gasp in shock, the air is knocked out of me. Virius flips me on my back and is over me. He tugs my pants down and is between my legs. He spreads my thighs wide, and then he's inside of me.

But not in the way I just asked for. I can't be bothered to mind as he makes good on his word—and I am coming while he's inside of me.

CHAPTER 11

VIRIUS

I warned her that prophecies are not always what they seem at face value. Words are passed down from one person to another. Translated into different languages, all of which have different meanings.

Zahara wanted me to be inside her while she came. I was happy to oblige in her pleasure. Only not with the part of me that she wanted.

With her naked and stripped bare, I shove my tongue into her cunny. No preamble. No light, little flicks. She didn't ask for that. She asked to have me inside her, and I am.

I have never done this myself. My tongue is a normal size. The women who paid to see me only wanted my cock and the unnatural tight fullness it could give them. They weren't interested in using or hearing from my mouth, so I've never performed oral sex. But I've seen it done many times.

I lift my head as I spread Zahara's thighs. Her cunny is a beautiful blush of dark pink. The ripest of berries.

Her scent makes me dizzy with want. The beast below stirs, throbbing and pulsing as I take her in. I've never had much control over my cock. It rose and fucked with its own mind. I would simply turn my mind off until it released into whatever woman was using it. Once it released and went limp, I slowly came back to myself. Until it stirred again, ready to service another.

I ignore it now as it throbs with need. I want this for myself. I don't want to zone out and miss a single second of Zahara. Not with her pretty mewls and her urgent pants. Her claws dig into my shoulders, enough so I bleed.

I should tell her to stop. But I don't. I like the thought of my blood on her. I want all to know that she is mine.

I put my nose right up to her flesh, and inhale. She is heaven. My fangs ache to take a bite of her and bring more of that ambrosia inside of myself.

"What are you doing?" she asks, her voice a mix of desire and uncertainty.

"I don't know," I admit. It's hard to form words over the throbbing of both my cock and my fangs.

"Were you about to bite me?"

I close my mouth, but it's impossible to swallow down the evidence of my desire.

"Don't," she says.

Her eyes flash with what I know is fear. Doesn't she know that I would rip out my fangs if I thought they would hurt her? Already, I'm contemplating castration.

I know Zahara wants my cock, but it can't give her what she wants. Vampires cannot create new life. My cock has nothing to give her. But I do.

I force my fangs back before I promise her, "I won't bite you."

Those are the last words that I am capable of forming. Zahara eyes me warily, but she is powerless to stop what is about to happen. She is a strong warrior, but I want to bring her to her knees. I wrap her knees at my ears and take another taste.

Zahara cries out. The sound of her fills my ears. The taste of her is on my tongue. My hands are full of her flesh as I hold her still.

I don't have to move my tongue much. She undulates her hips up and down. It's a tight rocking as I hold her torso.

I allow her the movements, thrilled to know that she likes what I am doing to her. I could lick her forever. I could gorge myself on the taste of her, the velvety feel of her flesh against my tongue.

The more I lick, the wetter she gets. The wetter she gets, the sweeter she tastes. Yes, this is heaven. I will fight any demon who dares to try to take me back to the hell of my prior existence.

I delve my tongue into her opening, so deep that my nose rests on her clit and my chin on her perineum. Zahara purrs, low and deep, more lioness than kitten. I know the sounds of pleasure, having heard them from women riding my cock. I also know the sounds of pain when they take too much of it. Zahara vocalizes only pleasure.

I push deeper inside, needing to fill her with all that I am. She stills as I swirl my tongue, gathering up every drop of her essence. A gasp fills my ears as she inhales sharply. Then there is a long, deep pulsing of her walls around my tongue. More wetness coats my tongue.

This taste is pure saccharine. It floods my senses and goes straight to my head, giving me a warm brain freeze. But the freeze thaws quickly as I swallow the honey down.

Zahara's cries continue as her body shivers. For an instant, I'm sure I feel fur and not flesh in my hands. Her moans turn to growls as she crests the height of her pleasure.

My own hips rock into the mattress as the beast demands

its due. It moves of its own accord, but the mattress is all it will get. I'm not sharing her with it.

I remove my tongue from her entrance and lap up the juices that have overflowed on her pussy's lips. My tongue latches onto the bud at the apex of her thighs, and I pull on the engorged flesh I find there.

Zahara cries out, a shuddery sound of pleasure. Her eyes flash that catlike gold at me again. I can see the panther in them, readying to rise. She shuts her eyes, and the image is gone.

I suckle the bud, and more of that exquisite moisture seeps out of her. Again, she is rocking against my tongue. I cover her mons with my entire mouth, and gulp her down.

The next time she cries out, there is a note of pain. I lift my head. Her eyes are glazed as the tremors tighten their hold on her. I know this look, too. She is drunk with pleasure. If I give her more, it could turn painful. I have watched women take more and come out sore. As much as it pains me, I back off from my delectable little treasure.

Bringing Zahara to my chest, I wrap her naked form inside my arms and cradle her. It's another thing that I have never experienced or have done to another, but I find it easy with her. Her wee body fits against my chest as if I was made for her. I'm coming to believe that I was. For the first time in my life, I feel that I have a sense of purpose.

She may be right. I do have a destiny. It is to pleasure and protect her. It's a future that I can say I look forward to.

Zahara falls asleep in my arms. My wee kitten can throw a punch, but she can't hold her pleasure. After her orgasms, she's out like a young buck who's busted a nut for the first time.

She curls into me with complete trust as she dozes. I feel strong having this warrior seek comfort in me. I want to give her everything she asks for. Perhaps there is a way for me to do so. There are rumors in the vampire world.

I hold my treasure close to my heart as I think. But the thinking doesn't get too far. My brain is far too addled for lack of blood. I'll have to do something about that sooner rather than later if I am to keep my promise of not biting her.

With great reluctance, I move Zahara off my chest and onto the cot. After pulling the sheet over her naked torso, I press a kiss to her temple. She doesn't stir as I move the door aside and walk out of the room. At the end of the path, I take the right turn that will lead me out of the cave.

CHAPTER 12

ZAHARA

My dreams are often those of running. Not those dreams where I'm running from zombies, or ducking to hide my nakedness from my classmates. I wish those were my dreams, but I've never been in a formal classroom.

No, my dreams aren't anything like the human dreams of running away. In my dreams, I run on all fours.

I'm climbing trees. Jumping in the water. My inner cat loves to play. She is often alone, as is the nature of a jaguar.

So it shocks me when I'm standing still in this dream. It shocks me even more that I'm standing on two legs instead of four. My face is tilted up as the sun kisses my eyelids, my nose, my mouth.

Then I feel another kiss. One made of flesh, not sunlight. I turn to find Virius standing in the light of the sun. I am inside the circle of his arms. The heat coming off his flesh rivals that of the sun. The smile on his face completely eclipses the star.

Damn, the man is beautiful even inside my mind. That wicked grin of his makes me press my thighs together beneath the threadbare sheets. I know what that mouth can do. That mouth is what sent me into dreamland way before my bedtime.

Like vampires, jaguars are nocturnal. Unlike vampires, we don't mind the sun. Which is when I finally note that my vampire is standing in the sunlight.

Something tells me to wake, that there is danger, as the sun moves across the sky. But Virius doesn't look up at it. He looks down. At my belly. My belly, which is full with a baby; his baby.

Again, my mind doesn't comprehend the logic. First a vampire in the sun. Now a baby in my belly after I was fingered and tongued. That's not how this works. Right?

The sun passes through clouds, casting a shadow around us. The shadows move across Virius's face and my belly.

Then the rays are back. They get closer and closer to him. I smell the acrid scent of burning flesh.

Virius's skin catches fire, but he doesn't appear to notice. His hand is on my belly. He smiles that unpracticed, lopsided grin at me as his skin burns away. The red flames eat at his honey-kissed skin. Black spots are all that is left behind as the sun's rays consume him.

And then, he is nothing. He is no one. And I am alone.

I wake up with a scream in my throat. I choke before the air can rush out of me. I inhale a gasp, trying to inflate my lungs, to call out.

Virius is not beside me. Before I'd fallen asleep, I remember being wrapped inside his arms. Now I'm alone in the cot, wrapped only in the pitiful excuse of a blanket. And he is gone.

I look frantically around the room. There is no sunlight from above. Nothing seeps through the cracks.

I look over to the door. There's a crack in its opening, as though it had been moved aside. There is only one person who could move that door aside with his bare hands.

My feet hit the ground before I realize I'm running. I slip through the crack in the door and dash down the narrow passageway. It doesn't dawn on me until I'm in the alcove that I'm naked.

I've never been shy of nudity. Animals don't wear clothes, and those that do dream of murdering the humans who dress them up in the shameful outfits. Shifting isn't like in the movies, where beings shift with their clothes fully intact. The proportions of woman and large cat are entirely different, so the threads will always stretch and break, regardless of how much either creature might diet.

But when I get to the alcove, the two women there look up and smirk at my nudity. Well, Zuma smirks as she looks me over. Pia purses her lips as she takes in my state of undress.

It takes me a second to realize why. Their ears are likely still ringing from what Virius was doing to me just a couple of hours ago.

"Where is he?" I demand.

"He left," they both say in unison.

My heart is pounding loudly in my ears, but not so loud that I miss the difference in inflection in their voices. Zuma's voice asks a question, as though she can't believe Virius would leave. Pia's tone of voice is more of a statement, like a confirmation of something she was waiting for.

I turn and focus on Pia. "You let him go?"

"He didn't come this way," she says.

But I can hear that there are words unsaid. Pia doesn't agree with how Itzel and the other elders are going about this matter. She has no love for vampires, but she believes that Virius should have a choice in how we proceed. Otherwise, it makes him a sacrifice.

"It sounded like you got what you needed from him," says Zuma.

My cheeks heat. Not because of what she heard, but because she's wrong about what she heard. I did not get what I needed from Virius. I didn't do what I was supposed to do with him to make a baby. But I don't want to explain that.

"Come and eat," says Zuma. "You must be famished after taking all of him on."

She winks a knowing eye at me. The trouble is, I don't know. I have no idea.

"I'll call the others," Zuma continues. "It's time to celebrate. The gods will be appeased."

"Don't," I say while turning towards the exit.

"Where are you going?" Pia calls after me.

"I'm going to find him."

"I don't blame you, sweetie," Zuma singsongs. "I'd tap that a couple more times if I were you, before his expiration date."

I have to force my panther to ignore her remarks. Zuma won't be tapping anything on Virius. He is mine. I just have to find my captive, and recapture him.

Stepping outside, I catch his scent. He hasn't gone far. I crouch down on two feet and let the panther take my body. With my nose to the ground, I find his trail. He won't escape me.

I'll catch him. And then what? Have my way with him, and set in motion his untimely death?

I have to. I don't have a choice. Neither of us do. Destiny is a bitch like that.

CHAPTER 13

VIRIUS

I peer down at the blood bag in my hand. It's my favorite type: B-negative. It's not from a typical blood bank, either. It's stock from Club Toxic. The label on the back of the bag says it was donated by a little sub named Layla, whose veins were tapped while she was being flogged.

Layla most definitely enjoyed her beating. The sweet aroma of the endorphins in the blood tickles my nose. But still, my mouth doesn't water at the thought of downing this sweet blood. My fangs feel limp at the thought of puncturing the plastic to get the life-giving blood into my sluggish veins.

There's only one vein I want to tap. Only one source I want to gorge myself on. But that spicket is resoundingly set to the *No* position.

Still, a man has to eat.

With my fangs uninterested, I grab a blade from the knife block. Using the pointy end of the steak knife, I punch a hole in the bag. When the trickle of blood hits my tongue, it's not as I expected.

Instead of the salty sweetness of the B-negative variety I've grown to love, the blood tastes like a mixture of sawdust and copper. I bend over the sink and spit it out. Turning on the faucet, I drown out the taste with hot water.

"What have I told you about leaving the refrigerator open?"

Peering through the running faucet water, I see Gaius standing in the doorway of the kitchen. He is dressed immaculately, as always. His suit is tailored to his body, not a thread or hair out of place. The elegance he cloaks himself in belies his birth, which was just as low as mine.

"For Fate's sake, Virius, it's the twenty-first century. Didn't we agree on modern clothing and not loincloths?"

"You escaped?" The feminine voice coming from behind Gaius belongs to his mate, Marechal. She is also covered in elegance. Her gown is a deep purple that matches her grape-colored eyes.

Marechal takes a step towards me. But before she reaches me, a shorter version of her flings herself into my arms.

"Viri, you escaped," says Cari as she crushes me to her.

Cari is a newly turned vampire. There is still a lot of strength in her untried limbs, enough that I cough and wheeze under her affectionate assault.

"Cari, let him go," says Hadrian. "Either you'll kill him with your strength, or I'll kill him because he has a hard-on while holding my wife."

All eyes go down to my crotch. Sure enough, the beast below stirs inside the loincloth. Cari jumps back as though the snake were preparing to strike. Marechal takes a step back as well.

"I thought you said you couldn't get it up anymore," says Hadrian as Cari returns to his side.

"I couldn't," I say. "Until her."

"Me?" asks Cari, pointing a finger at her chest.

"No, Zahara. It wants her. It wants her badly. I've been hard all day. My balls have actually turned bl—"

"Virius!" Both Hadrian and Gaius hold up their hands as they shout.

I move my hand away from the knot of the toga where I had intended to untie the fabric to show them my agony and shame.

"I don't know what to do," I say.

Marechal's brows rise as she dips her mouth to Gaius's ear. "Have you two had The Talk?"

Her voice is a whisper. She has only been in the vampire world for a few days. She doesn't seem to realize that our hearing is exceptional.

"Trust me," Cari says to me, "you don't want Mare to give you The Talk."

"I give a great talk," Marechal harrumphs. "I did fine with you and Arneis."

"Sure," says Cari. "And now look at us. All mated to vampires—"

"Virius," Gaius cuts his wife and sister-in-law off. "What happened with you and the shifter?"

"She wants a child."

"Can…" Cari stops and starts. "Can vampires have children?"

"No, *minou*." Hadrian presses a kiss to her temple. Regret is heavy on his brow.

"That's not entirely true," says Gaius. "It has happened before."

"You mean Dom?" says Hadrian.

Gaius nods. I note that his brows are heavy as well. But not with regret, with concern. His lips are set in a firm line.

It's the look he gives when he wants to keep something from me.

"Who's Dom?" I ask. "A vampire? He has a child? Do you know how he did it?"

Gaius holds up his hands as though that motion could stop my questions. "All I know is that he has a child with a human woman, and that the birth came at a cost."

"So, it is possible?"

"We don't know what the costs are." Gaius sighs.

"It doesn't matter. I'll pay whatever to give my mate what she wants."

"You're mated?" says Gaius. "It's barely been twenty-four hours."

"And how soon did you know Marechal was yours?"

Gaius purses his lips. Then his features relax as he turns to the woman he handed over the keys to his private sex dungeon in Club Toxic for.

"And you with Cari," I say to Hadrian.

Hadrian pulls Cari to him. His arms wrap around the woman who fell from the sky and into his arms. He hasn't let the little daredevil go since that skydiving accident, which turned out to be his good fortune.

"You love her?" asks Gaius.

"I don't know what that is," I say.

I thought I'd loved my mother, but she sold me into a life of sexual slavery without a backward glance. True, it was always going to be my fate to be a whore. But under any other *lena* of my time, it would have been for only one lifetime. Belonging to Domitia put my body in servitude for many lifetimes.

I know what it means to survive. I know what it means to serve. But to love?

"You love Marechal," I say to Gaius. "What does it feel like?"

"It feels like…" He looks down at Marechal. She smiles up at him, waiting patiently for his response. "It feels like what I remember sunshine to be. When she's in a room, it feels like the sun is shining on my face."

Tears sparkle at the corners of Marechal's eyes. Gaius dips his head to capture the drops before they fall.

I can't remember what sunshine feels like. So, I have no idea what he means. I look out through the glass patio door and into the dark night.

A shadow moves out of the foliage. Eyes flash at me, like lightning streaking across a stormy sky. A large black cat comes up to the glass. Its eyes are intent on me. Its fangs glisten in the moonlight.

"I think it's for you," says Gaius.

I walk up to the door and pull the latch. Once the door is open, the jaguar transforms into a woman.

Zahara stands naked on the other side of the door. She is streaked with mud up and down her calves. There are scratches from vines on her forearms. But her breasts are untouched, the nipples erect and begging for a taste.

My thirst increases at the sight of them. I also feel dizzy with the low blood count I'm working with. I ignore my organs' needs in favor of my desire for her.

I need to get my hands on her. But when I reach for her, the claws come out. She smacks my hand away, leaving four bloody marks.

"You left me," she says as she stomps inside.

Her muddy feet leave tracks on the floor. I know Gaius will be pissed. But he stays silent behind me. The silence gives me a second to replay Zahara's words.

"I would never leave you."

"I woke up. You were gone. Meaning: you left me."

"I got hungry." I point to the bag of blood on the counter.

Zahara doesn't spare my evidence a glance. She jabs the

claw of her index finger into my bare chest, drawing out another stream of blood.

"You. Are. My. Captive." She enunciates every word with a puncturing poke.

I should feel pain. But with each poke, I feel like she's breaking through a dense fog. Each fissure in my chest feels like a ray of sunlight brightening me from the inside out. Is this love?

"Your captive?" I capture her hand and press it into my bloody chest, right over my heartbeat. "Right. I forgot. I didn't want to wake you. I thought that last orgasm you had would've put you out for longer."

A flush spreads across Zahara's cheeks and her eyes dart over my shoulder at the crowd behind us. She stands naked before them, but it's the mention of her orgasms that makes her blush.

"I figured I'd be back before you woke up," I say in my defense.

"That's not how imprisonment works."

"I'll tell you the next time before I leave, okay?"

"Fine." The word is said in exasperation, like there is no fight left in her. She looks exhausted.

I gather her body into my arms. She doesn't fight me. She rests her head under my chin as I walk her out of the kitchen and head to my bedroom.

"You're dirty. Let me clean you up."

CHAPTER 14

ZAHARA

The water is cool on my toes. A stream of current rushes towards my ankles, rising up to massage my calf muscles. I sigh as I sink down into the depths, then yelp when I feel the jets.

Back home, I often bathed in the hot springs surrounding an active volcano. But the lava had nothing on the powered steam in this tub. For one, there are no craggy rocks at my back. This tub is cushioned. My feet don't sink into silt but instead rest on cool porcelain. When I look up, I see another familiar sight: a tall, dark mountain. This peak is capped with sandy blond hair instead of angry red fire.

Virius leans over the tub. His large, thick fingers massage the soap into a cloth. The scent is divine. He bids me lean forward. When I do as he asks, he puts the cloth on my back and begins to scrub.

I only barely stop myself from mewling. A purr escapes my throat. A shudder runs over my shoulder blades. I only just stop myself from arching in the tub and offering him my belly. Because what I truly want to do is go on all fours and lift my tail for him.

How is it that I've wound up naked in the bathroom of my prisoner? I'm the one weaponless and at his mercy as he breaks down all my defenses with a bar of exotic smelling soap?

I can't find it in me to be chagrined. I have absolutely no intention of getting out of this predicament. For so much of my life, I have been revered as someone who would bring about a revolution. But no one has ever tended to me in this manner. No one has ever treated me like I was precious. I may have been tasked by the Fates, but this is the first time I've felt worship.

And I like it.

The water sluices down my body. Bubbles form and pop, and run down my skin in rivulets. Virius's hand follows the downpour, making a waterfall from my shoulder caps. I shiver as the droplets run over the mounds of my breasts.

"Is it too hot?" he asks.

"It's perfect," I sigh.

"You're perfect," he says.

Taking my hand, he scrubs each of my fingertips. The care and concentration he gives each nail is more attention than anyone has paid me—the actual me and not the me in a prophecy—in my whole life. I want to run out and dig my fingers into the dirt just to have Virius clean them again. Negative attention is still attention, and I want any form of attention this man will give me.

But I don't have to run out and make a mess to hold Virius's attention. My hands are only a starting block. He runs the cloth over my face next.

"Close your eyes," he says.

If he had said these words to me a few hours ago, I would

have snorted and palmed my dagger. Now I tilt my head back and do as he commands. My reward is swift. With one hand, Virius cradles my chin in his palm. With the other, he gently wipes away the stress of the night, of the last day, of the last few years of my life.

He wipes each eyelid. The sides of my nose. The space above my upper lip. He scrubs behind my ears. The back of my neck.

By the time he reaches my breasts, I am shivering with need. I know he must feel it too. But when I open my eyes to check, his face is a mask of focus and concentration.

"Get in the tub with me," I say.

"Is that another order?" He says it with a grin at the corner of his mouth.

He should know better than to play with a cat. He's dangling a ball of yarn in front of the face of a feline who has sharp claws.

Instead of lashing out to get what I want, I whisper, "Please?"

That catches him off guard. His hand stills. His jaw works as he swallows something thick down his throat.

The cloth falls into the tub. The white fabric is flung to the center when it hits the jets. Then it sinks down to the bottom in surrender.

Slowly, Virius stands. He's dressed only in the makeshift loincloth of his tattered clothing. I watch as he tugs at the knot of the toga. It doesn't take much force for his cock to spring free. Frankie must've been working the lock of his imprisonment from the inside.

Virius cups himself. His hands aren't big enough to cover the beast he's un-toga'd. "Remember what I said."

I nod, though I have no idea what we're talking about. I'm too hypnotized by the single eye of his cock.

I'd felt Frankie pressed against me earlier. But seeing him

again... well, damn. I forgot how truly massive that monster was.

Virius's cock is easily the width of my forearm, and as long. There truly is no way that anaconda is fitting inside me. So why do my thighs press together at the possibility?

Viri steps into the tub behind me. His body weight displaces the water and it sloshes on the ground. I wonder how much of that displacement comes from what he carries between his thighs.

I turn so that I'm facing him. Digging around in the water, I find the washcloth of surrender. I raise that sudsy white flag and begin scrubbing him.

He watches me warily, and then with growing curiosity, as though no one has ever bathed him before. Then I remember what he said about his mother.

"Have you always wanted to be a mother?" he asks.

I'm shocked by his question. I don't go with my normal answer of, *it's my destiny*. Because in the past forty-eight hours, he's made me feel like I have a choice—though I know that I don't.

"Doesn't every woman?" I reply.

I curse under my breath at the insensitivity of my words. By his account, his mother did not want him. Had, in fact, sold him into slavery.

"I'm sorry," I say.

"For what?" Virius leans into my touch, much like a big cat would. "Oh, you mean my mother?"

He inhales deeply, his nose an inch away from my hair. He holds that breath for a long time. His exhale sounds reluctant. When he opens his eyes, he takes the cloth from me and pulls me into his arms. He turns my body so that my back is to his front. As he fits me into the cradle of his form, I feel him adjust Frankie. But there's not much adjusting he can do. I feel the impression of his cock against my spine. My temperature rises against the warm cocoon of his chest.

"She could've left me on the street when I was pulled from her womb, but she didn't."

My hackles rise at the mention of another woman on Virius's lips. Then I remember what I'd asked him only a moment ago. He's talking about his mother.

"She brought me inside. She left food for me... sometimes. It was always clear that I would need to fend for myself. I just..."

He stays silent for a long time. Part of my brain isn't interested in his words, it's too focused on the warmth radiating from his body. He is hotter than the stream of the water from the jets. I want to know more about this man. I want both the light and the dark pieces of him.

"You just what?"

"If my mother had asked me to, I would've chosen to go with Domitia, to help her to become free."

"Domitia is the one who enslaved you?"

Behind me, Virius's muscles tense. Frankie stops his incessant pulsing and actually slackens against my back. "I don't like her name on your lips."

"I don't like that she tried to break you."

"She didn't try. She did break me. I'm not a whole man; I know that. I wasn't born with all my faculties. Then becoming the favored pet to a sadist didn't help matters."

"There's nothing wrong with you. You didn't do anything wrong. There were bad people in your life who were supposed to protect you. They're the broken ones."

"I would do it all again if it would lead me to you."

I turn to face him. His gaze is hooded, but he hides nothing. The look in his eyes is just far away, as though he's trapped in memories.

I need to pull him back. I want him in the present, with

me. This man has been through unimaginable pain. He should be raging against the world. Instead, he holds me gently in his arms.

I want to hold him too. But not in his arms. I reach down into the water and find the thick mass of flesh between us.

Virius hisses as my fingertips graze his cock. His large hand cups mine, readying to push it away.

"Please," I say. "Please, let me touch you."

CHAPTER 15

VIRIUS

It is the *please* that does it. No one has ever begged me for anything. Except for their life.

Zahara knows I will never harm a hair on her head. I have proven to her that I only seek her happiness, her security, her well-being. Hell, I laid my fortune at her feet within a few hours of meeting her. And still, all she has asked of me is the one thing I am loath to give to her.

Please, let me touch you.

No one has ever asked. All my life, things have only been taken from me. And the thing most taken has been what lies between my thighs. So, I hesitate when Zahara asks permission. Being the warrior that she is, she takes my hesitation for compliance. With the first touch of her fingertip against the beast, he strikes out.

My body is sent careening in two diverging directions. My back arches as though I've been struck by lightning. But the rod is coming from me. It's the beast crash landing in the other direction. It bolts right into Zahara's palm.

My mind explodes as I try to put the pieces of my shattered consciousness back together. A thick fog settles all around me as sensations pour down from a thunderstorm of emotions. I try to move my legs, to lift my arms. It feels impossible.

The only thing that I can feel is a heatwave of pressure coming from my groin area. Looking down, I expect to see that my cock is on fire. The thought of my cock being burned off doesn't concern me. It'll take a while for the organ to regenerate. In that time, I can have peace of mind as I lie with Zahara, knowing that for a few days, it can't harm her.

As the fog in my mind slowly clears, I see that there are no flames between my thighs. There is golden flesh against my own. A hand.

The fingers of that hand are long, but not slender. The nails are chipped and ragged, entirely unlike the manicured hands of my regular clientele. But the fingers are female.

Zahara.

She's touching me with those working woman's hands. I feel the calluses on her thumb as she strokes downward. That rough piece of skin lags and catches on my glans at the tip. The contact causes my balls to tighten. As they do, a coil of heat tightens in them, pulling at the skin around the beast, causing it to tighten and I gasp.

"Oh Fates, did I hurt you?" Zahara moves her hand from my cock.

I let out a harsh breath. Not one of relief. One of need. For once, both the beast and I are in agreement. We need her hand back on our flesh.

"I've never done this before. Am I doing it wrong? I want to make you feel as good as you made me feel."

Her words are all a jumble. It will take too much concentration to try and understand them. I don't have enough blood to divert to my head. All the fluid in my body has rushed down to the throbbing flesh between my thighs.

"Show me what to do. Show me how you touch yourself when you masturbate."

Masturbate? I've never done it. Why would I want to rouse that monstrous part of me?

"Oh, I know what I'm missing. Lube," she says.

I'm cognizant enough to watch as Zahara picks up the soap I used to clean her body. She rubs her hands together to build lather. Then she places not one but both hands on me.

"*Fuuuuuutuo.*" I bellow the ancient Roman curse.

The thunderstorm is back. It has brought with it furies from the seas. The avenging spirits come to life inside me and whip up a frenzy in my lower belly. Electricity crackles everywhere Zahara's fingers touch my cock, as though my blood and the mythological creatures are trying to get out of my flesh to get to hers.

What magic is this woman wielding over me? All thoughts of stopping her have left my mind. There isn't much left in there aside from getting closer to her.

"Is that better?"

Better? I had no idea that any good could come to me from my cock. No, this isn't better. This is the best thing that has ever happened to me.

I peer down into the water. My cock can be clearly seen through the suds of the bath. The red tip doesn't appear angry. It strains with the same objective: it's eager to get closer to her. The veins running along the sides of my flesh move and pulse to Zahara's strokes. Even my balls coil and tighten, pulling up closer to get nearer to her as she comes close to the root of me.

I finally understand the meaning of the saying: *she has him by the balls.* My balls have been had by hundreds of women, thousands. But not a single one of them ever had me. I never felt anything more than stiff as they impaled themselves on my shaft, followed by a moment of relief after my seed spilled.

With Zahara's hands on me, I feel the seed building inside of me. I feel a low heat in my back that pulses in time with the rhythm of her strokes. It comes from the beast, a promise of pleasure that it's sharing with me.

For hundreds of years, I've been cut off from feeling any of this. My mind would always shut down when my cock became erect to do its duty. But now... now, I want this.

I want to be with Zahara. I want to be around her. I want to be a part of her. I want to be inside of her.

My hips begin to thrust my cock into her hand, seeking more friction. I want to shake the suds off her hands. Even that thin layer of lubrication is too much space between us.

I reach out to her. Her flesh is hot in the cool waters of the bath. My hands slide down to cup the globes of her lush ass as she settles her knees over my hips. There is barely an inch between us, only enough space for her hand around my thick cock.

For a moment, I panic. Worry creases my brow as I look down. But my cock doesn't try to worm itself into her sheath.

It stands erect between our bellies, its single eye focused squarely up and on Zahara as she handles it.

"Good?" she asks, speeding up her strokes.

I can't answer. I can't remember the English language. It would take too much to remember the single-syllabled word for agreement. So, I nod my head in the universal language of *fuck, yeah*.

With two hands, Zahara strokes long and firm, from the base of my cock all the way up to the tip. I am uncircumcised, but there is no give in my taut foreskin. I can feel the lifelines on her palms. I can feel the grooves where her fingers meet her palm, then bend at the knuckle, and the ones just before her fingertips.

She circles the fat head of my erection and it weeps into her hand. The pre-cum catches in the lifelines of her palm before being washed away by the cool water. Just that small release has me shuddering.

My gaze is half-lidded, but my eyes are open enough to see Zahara grinning. My heart skips a beat at the sight. Domitia grinned whenever she thought of a new heinous way to inflict pain.

Zahara is not Domitia. Zahara smiles because she likes my pleasure. She is the only one to offer any to me.

My arms circle around Zahara's back. I pull her to me, needing to be surrounded by her. The bright smell of her. The fiery taste of her. The light in her eyes.

She is sunlight to me, exactly as I remember it. Warm rays on my face. Soft heat cradling my back. A glow that halos around me even after I've closed my eyes or gone inside.

I now understand what Gaius meant. I'm sure of what this is that I'm feeling. I want to tell her, but there is an urgent need that cuts the line of my declaration.

The tension inside me is at breaking point. I am a dam ready to burst if just one more droplet of water falls on me. I am a balloon ready to pop with just a whisper of air.

Zahara strokes down.

Everything inside of me, everything that I've held behind protective walls, breaks free.

Surprisingly, the tension doesn't loosen from my cock-head first. It starts in my hips. The warm tidal wave rushes inward, to my groin area. The spasms start in my balls as they tighten, releasing hold of my essence.

This has all happened to me thousands of times, but this is the first time I've been present for the performance. As my seed rushes up my erection, my arms and legs go numb. My head feels light as even more fluid is pulled from there. My balls throb as my cock begins to pump its release.

Zahara's grin spreads even wider as she sees the fruits of her labor. Her eyes flash, like a cat's who just found the cream. Her delight is too bright. She's a shining star that twinkles down at me. The only reason I am tethered to this plane of existence is because she still has a hold on me. If she moves her hand from my dick, I'm sure I will fall, sink down into the depths of the tub, and drown.

It would be a good death. But I don't want to leave her. I want to be with her forever.

As I pump my last bit of seed, I feel as though I have died. But I am reborn.

A sweet heat remains as my dick goes flaccid in Zahara's hand. For the first time in my life, the beast has been tamed. The connection between myself and that piece of flesh remains. We are both content and sated.

For now.

CHAPTER 16

ZAHARA

The darkness surrounding me is thick and absolute. But I'm not afraid. It's the warmest, most safe place to be.

My body feels rested and relaxed. My mind is at ease from a dreamless sleep. My empty stomach is too content to growl and demand it be filled.

I feel... happy.

Such a strange feeling. I'm surprised to realize I haven't felt it in years. Have I ever truly felt it before?

I'm not sure. I'm starting to think I haven't.

No, I have never felt this bubbly sensation that makes me want to smile at nothing in particular.

Can't say that my toes have ever wiggled as though they couldn't wait to dance to a song that has no particular beat.

And my hands, they want to reach out and grasp at something. The desire to be full of that something is so enormous that it pulls my eyes open.

Having my eyes wide open is no different than being asleep. The darkness surrounding me in my wakefulness is also absolute. But I know where I am. I know whose body lies next to mine. I know whose hand holds mine.

Virius.

He sleeps like the dead beside me. Though his fingers are entwined with mine, he isn't holding on to me. I can't hear him breathing, because he isn't. Vampires have little need for air, only enough to circulate the stolen blood in their systems.

Slowly, bits of his features come into view. First, the bright blond of his golden hair. That, I can see clearly. But the strong chin, the broken nose, the lush lips, those I can place only because they are ingrained in my memory.

I don't know this man. Not truly. But lying beside him, in the dark room, I feel closer to him than I have any other person in my life.

And just like everything I truly want for myself, I can't have him. Guilt stabs me in the chest—the thought that fulfilling my destiny will mean the end of his life. But I've been taught that the needs of the many outweigh the few.

Virius Serrano is just one person. Not even a person. He's a vampire. He's lived for hundreds of years. But by all accounts, not much of his life has been good.

I am a fool to think I'm doing him a courtesy by ending his miserable life. Because the last couple of days have not felt like misery. Not to hear him tell it. Not my experience of it with him.

The feelings of warmth and safety only magnify as I rest my chin on his chest. I still want to dance, only slower now. I want him to sway me back and forth in his arms as we try to outrun the clock of inevitability. I can't stop what's coming. Fate will have her due. All I can do is make the best of the time we have.

As I lie against his chest, straining to see more of him in the darkness of the setting sun, the smallest of inhales whistles into Viri's nose. It happens only once in a few minutes. It proves he's alive.

My internal clock tells me that the sun is setting. So why isn't he up?

In the silence of the room, my stomach grumbles. My bladder also calls my attention. I extricate myself from my lover and head back to the bathroom to take care of the necessaries.

Inside the bathroom, I turn on the light. The woman who looks back at me in the mirror isn't entirely unrecognizable. But she does look different.

Her hair is a rat's nest of tangles. Her lips are swollen from the long, endless kisses Virius gave after his hand job. I suspect he kept kissing me even after I fell asleep inside his arms.

I have a lover. A strong man who delights in my pleasure. A gentle giant who doesn't trust his own strength. I vow that, for however much time we have left, I'm going to show Virius nothing but pleasure. I'm going to show him nothing but kindness. I owe him that much.

I wrap myself up in his robe before leaving the bathroom. In the bedroom, I see he still hasn't stirred. But my belly is now demanding its due.

I slip out of the room, careful not to let any of the sun's setting light spill inside to harm him. That precaution wasn't necessary. There are no windows in the hall.

When I make my way back to the kitchen, I see that the sun has nearly set. Only a few rays straggle behind on the horizon, as though they are naughty children who don't want to be put to bed.

I startle when I see Hadrian Serrano standing to the side

of the patio door. His hand reaches out to one of the rays. It burns the tip of his finger.

"Doesn't that hurt?"

He doesn't startle at the sound of my voice. Like shifters, vampires have excellent hearing. I'm sure he heard me coming from the hallway. Unless the bedrooms are sound-proofed, he likely heard both Virius and me coming last night.

"Yes, it does." He brings his smoking finger back towards his body and studies it.

"Then why are you doing it?"

He lifts his gaze and regards me. "It reminds me of what I have to live for."

The fingertip heals instantly. Hadrian gives it a shake as though he just blew out a match. The sun has completely receded down into the horizon, and only the moon's light remains.

Hadrian crosses to the refrigerator. He pulls the leftovers of a steak from the appliance's belly, and sets the dish before me, with a knife and fork.

"Thank you," I say, digging in.

"Once, I only thought about ways to die," he says, as though picking up on the end of a conversation I wasn't aware we were having. "That was when I thought I'd lost the love of my life."

I know he's talking about his sire, Domitia. I know that sadistic bitch didn't only whore out Virius. I heard she did atrocious things to Hadrian in the twisted name of love.

"You know Domitia used to rip my heart out. Literally."

Damn, so those rumors were true. I had assumed they were hyperbole.

"She got her hands around my heart, but she got her hooks in Viri's head. She's still in there." Hadrian knocked on the side of his head. "I need to know if you mean him any harm."

The piece of steak I'm chewing doesn't go down right. Hadrian pours me a glass of water and waits for me to clear my throat. Once I have my voice back, I tell him the truth.

"Virius is my destiny. It was foretold that we would be together."

"And have a child?"

I nod, not willing to say any more. Not willing to give anything else away, including the little time I'll have with Viri.

"You understand that prophecies are not always what they seem?"

So Virius has said. And I know that the Mayans predicted the end of the world—and that that date came and went a decade ago, and we are all still standing.

"He's signed over his stake in the vineyard to you," Hadrian continues. "As a mating present. Gaius and I are prepared to do the same."

This time I do choke, even though there's no meat or water in my mouth. Hadrian watches me impassively. His shrewd gaze studies me like a predator waiting to see in which direction its prey will bolt.

I sit still. "Thank you for the gift. But it's still Virius I need."

A slow grin spreads across Hadrian's handsome face. I suppose that's the answer he wants, the answer that doesn't make me out to be a gold digger. Little does he know it's not gold I'm after.

"Take this." He hands me what looks like a juice pouch, only the fluid inside isn't filled with color dye and sugar. "Virius will be hungry when he wakes."

I hold the blood in my hand and frown down at it. The white label at the top of it reads *B-negative*. Instead of the word *Volunteer Donor*, there is an emblem with a logo for Club Toxic on the bag. A woman's name is printed in a cursive font. *Layla*, it reads, followed by the words: *flogged for thirty minutes.*

I know vampires need blood to live. I also know that the blood is a delicacy when endorphins are released in a human. One of the best ways to bring about that flood is through sexual pleasure.

"That's his favorite," Hadrian says. His lips are curled in a challenge.

I wolf down the last piece of the steak and slide off the counter. With the moon rising in the sky, I head back to the bedroom. Back to my man. Layla is left behind on the counter. Hopefully, her sweet blood will turn rancid and inedible in the room temperature of the kitchen.

CHAPTER 17

VIRIUS

I'm always up the moment the last ray of the sun sets. It's a habit from when I was first turned into a vampire. I knew my fate soon after I was sold to Domitia by my mother.

Domitia had always been a bit of a drama queen. There were rumors that she had tried to take the stage in Ancient Greece as a human. But when it was found out that she was a woman, she had been kicked off and then shunned. Her theatrical flares were then turned towards the men she turned.

I wasn't the first child she'd collected and groomed before turning. Clodius, whom Domitia had taken when he was a babe in arms, had a fear of beds. Even after he was turned into a lethal creature of the night, he slept standing up to ensure no monsters could reach up and grab him.

With me, Domitia liked to play a game of hide and seek. She didn't look for me with her eyes. When she found me, she didn't grab me with those razor-sharp nails of hers and say: *Gotcha*. No, she liked to hunt me with a torchlight so bright, I thought it was the sun.

I knew what the sun did to vampires. Each morning before I went to sleep, Domitia would send me off to dreamland with the promise of turning me in my sleep. In the evening, when I woke, she'd shine the bright torchlight in my face, making me think I was a turned vampire who would burn.

Now, every evening when I wake, slowly peeling open one eye to check for light, I can still hear her cackling.

Inside my bedroom, it is too dark even for shadows. Not a sliver of light has made its way inside. But I know I'm not alone.

I can't see her, but I can smell her. Not the earthy scent of turned earth that always clings to her skin. Not the lush, sweet smell of a ripe grape. Not the musky scent of her wet cunny.

What I smell above all that is the sweet fatty acids, the bitter iron, and savory proteins of Zahara's blood. Hunger grips me. The few blood cells that remain inside me all rush to my gut. I have never had to fight against that particular organ before, as a vampire. The stranglehold it wraps around me is Herculean compared to my cock.

My dick doesn't rouse as I snatch Zahara from her post at the door. Her abundant curves are light in my arms as I toss her down onto the bed. She lets out a yelp of surprise. My hands are pinning her down before she can escape me. My dick remains tame, still sated, even with her sweet cunny so near. It's my fangs that have become the real monster. Those sharp points are the new beast that will take its due.

My fangs punch through my gums. The four points of pain don't bring me back to my senses. Zahara's wide eyes do.

They flash up at me—not one, but two suns shining on me in the night. Zahara's gaze is brighter than any torch Domitia ever used to bring on nightmares. I see the truth in Zahara's stare; I am the monster.

I release my hold on her. Once she is free, Zahara sits up. She reaches over to the nightstand and turns on the lamp there.

Soft illumination floods the room. But the glare of the light is too much for me. I move to the end of the bed, preparing to put as much distance between her and myself.

And I thought I could be a father? I can't control my most base instincts. Not my dick. Not my fangs. There is no way I can be trusted with a new life, even if creating one were possible.

Zahara's hand catches my wrist before I can get far. "Where are you going?"

I don't answer. I can't. Shame clogs my throat and clouds my eyes.

"To the kitchen?" she continues when I remain mute. "To grab a bag of Layla?"

I have to turn to her now. Her words aren't making any sense to me. What's a Layla?

"I don't want you drinking sex-spiked blood anymore," Zahara goes on. "If you're thirsty, you'll drink from me."

Either I'm asleep and dreaming the cruelest nightmare, or I'm awake and hallucinating. I'm not sure which I'd prefer to be true. Zahara is slipping out of her robe. Her naked body is revealed to me as she peels off the pieces of fabric. There is an ache in my loins. But the low levels of blood in my gut refuse to go any further south, so my cock can't rise to do anything about my mate's nakedness.

So, this is a nightmare then.

"I just nearly killed you," I finally manage some words.

"You mean when you tossed me on the bed?" Zahara

moistens her lips, leaving behind a glossy grin. "I thought that was foreplay."

Not a nightmare. Perhaps a very vivid fantasy?

"You're thirsty," she continues. It isn't a question. "I'm giving you permission to drink me."

The pounding in my fangs dampens the throbbing of my cock. I move towards her. Slowly. Not because I fear I'll scare her. I'm scared of myself.

My need for this woman is great, so absolute. Every part of me wants a part of her. My teeth want to sink into her veins. My cock wants to thrust into her sheath. My eyes want to feast upon her loveliness. I need to touch her with my tongue, taste her with my hands, get the smell of her on my teeth.

"Spread your thighs for me, my wee kitten."

With only a hint of hesitation, which I suspect comes from the endearment and not my command, Zahara does as she's told. She opens to me. My gaze has trouble focusing as the heat of desire washes over me. The gates of Heaven are open to me. Two paths lie ahead.

The first gate is a set of double doors. The pink lips of her cunny are flushed red with the evidence of her desire for me. I could sink my tongue into her entrance and sate the cravings of my loins.

On both sides of the first gate sits the other set of doors. Her femoral arteries are the blood supply that is pumping in the blood fueling Zahara's sexual thirst I could sink my fangs into one of those thighs and sate my blood thirst.

She's offering me both. Where should I start?

I take a step towards her. My gaze flicks from her dripping cunny to the pulsing beat of the blood beneath her skin. I wrap a hand around her right ankle. With my rough tug, Zahara collapses flat onto her back.

I spread her thighs out, like a butterfly opening its wings.

Using my thumb, I brush through the curls of her sex to find her bud. It's already swollen, filled with the essence she has offered me for my sustenance.

I swipe at it, rubbing her clit in tight circles. Once Zahara is purring from the attention, I give the bud a lick.

Just a taste. It is only the appetizer. And like all appetizers, the bite-sized sample of her clitoris does not fill me.

Slipping two fingers into her tight cunny, I pump my fingers in time to the blood rushing through her artery. In no time, she is trembling, crying out her pleasure to me. The moment I feel her walls clenching around my fingers, I sink my teeth into her thigh.

Zahara screams as I pull. The dual sensations are likely causing a duel inside her. The muscle-clenching pleasure of the orgasm. The piercing bliss that comes from my bite.

I can taste the change in her blood as the endorphins flood her system. It's the difference between taking no lumps of sugar in a cup of tea and drinking a little bit of tea leaves from the sugar dish. The saccharine taste of her doesn't rush to my head. It rushes to my groin. The beast wants in on the action. With my mind clear and my veins full, I can't fathom why that isn't a good idea.

CHAPTER 18

ZAHARA

I'm not sure how long I shake. I'm not sure how long I tremble. I can't remember a time when my body was still. When my insides weren't hot and clenching.

Why do people bother getting out of bed in the morning —or at any time of the day, for that matter? This is how I want to spend the rest of my life: having Virius Serrano bring me to orgasm with his mouth, his fingers, and now with his fangs.

I can't blame Layla the blood donor for volunteering anymore. Had I known the bliss of a bite, I would have lined up outside Club Toxic myself. But she can't have Virius' fangs. He's my man, and the hell if I'll share.

I look up at my man through glazed eyes. His lips are coated with a gloss of red. I grin to know it's my blood.

He licks at the droplets on his lower lip, but a sheen remains. It's not just my blood that paints his lips. It's also the result of my back-bending orgasm.

"I want more," I say. "I want all of you."

I reach for his dick. I expect Virius to step back, to grab my wrists and pin me down. I wouldn't have minded that. I've grown to like being overpowered by him. If another man or beast had tried it, I would have had their balls.

I want Virius's balls. I want them slapping against my ass as he thrusts into me. And I think I might just get my wish.

Virius doesn't pull away from me as I grab for Frankie. He leans into my touch. Maybe he'll let me give him another hand job? I'll settle for that tonight. But tomorrow he's going to have to give me the real deal. He won't have a choice.

Tomorrow night is the lunar eclipse. Neither of us can stop that celestial occurrence. And when it happens, the prophecy will be due.

But I don't want to think about that. I just want to think of him. I just want to make this man feel happy, to feel whole for as long as we have together.

Virius folds his large hand around mine. We are holding his shaft between us, together.

"I can't get you pregnant," he says.

"That's why I want you now. Because I want you. I don't want this to be about destiny or duty. I want it to be about me and you. Please."

His lids shut, and his body shudders.

"Please," I say again. "I want you."

Viri's lips capture mine. His tongue strokes against mine. I taste the metallic tint of my blood and the musky undertones of my orgasm. I am laid out on the bed with his large body covering mine. And still, it's not enough.

His long, cock is still in my hand. The width of him is so thick that my fingers don't meet as they wrap around his girth. Viri lets out a guttural moan as I try to angle him downward to my entrance. He shudders when my fingers graze the blunt tip of his cockhead.

There is a war waging on his face. His gaze is heavy-lidded with desire. His lips are pinched together with wariness.

I decide then and there I'm going to win this war. With my free hand, I give him a push. Like a large teddy bear, he rolls over to his back. Like the hunter I am, I mount my quarry.

Spreading my thighs, I straddle Virius. Though I've always been a flexible girl, the stretch to get my legs to span his hips is a bit of a challenge. But it's one I'm up for.

Viri looks up at me with wide eyes. His gaze is no longer heavy-lidded. It burns so brightly, it feels like the sun is on me.

I position myself over his groin. I could probably balance my full body weight on his erection. But that's not what I want to do with the stiff rod at my disposal. I want that monster inside me. And I want it now.

I rub my bare sex against the tip of his cock. He sucked my labia dry after taking my blood, but I am again dripping with need for him.

When I fit Viri's cock at my entrance, I have second thoughts. Even as I move my hips to adjust, I keep slipping to one side or the other, leaving a part of his thickness on the outside of my entrance.

Viri's jaw is clenched as he watches me. He doesn't stop me. His gaze is so clouded over with desire, I don't think he can.

Finally, after the world's slowest belly dance shimmy, I manage to fit the entire head at my entrance. The skin there protests as it stretches. But it doesn't hurt, not exactly.

The stretch feels good. It feels right. It feels like... destiny.

I lean over and kiss Viri. Still rubbing myself against him. Still trying to ease my way in.

"Zahara," he says in a hushed tone. "You are like sunlight."

"You haven't seen the sun in hundreds of years."

"My memories of it are nowhere near as bright as you."

I smile at that. A vampire called me his sun. A tear pricks my right eye, but I don't let it fall.

Whatever happens after this, I want to be with this man tonight. I want to give him what I've been saving all my life. I want to share my body with him. Not because I have to, but because I want to.

I sink down further. It's a series of fits and starts. There's nothing sexy about the mechanics of fitting Virius's big penis into my tight pussy. But as I descend down onto him, I feel like I'm rising.

He is a tight fit—so tight, I have trouble getting air into my lungs. Viri not only fills my channel, he also fills my mind; my heart. He's quickly tapping into my soul.

My body sinks lower onto his. I feel the veins on his cock against my walls. I feel the head pulsing. I feel his balls tightening against my ass as I come to sit.

His breath is my breath. His hands hold me tight. His eyes do not leave mine.

For all that I diss the spiritual, this feels like we're on a different plane of existence.

I am shuddering as he slides deeper into me. His hands come around me. He pulls me closer to him until there is not an inch between us.

I am his. And he is mine. The curtains close to block out any hint of the celestial bodies intruding in on us. But inside, I explode, and tiny shards of light dance behind my eyelids as I orgasm around the fullness of him. The fullness of me.

When the shuddering stops, I see that we've only just begun. Slowly, Virius withdraws his cock. It's only by a few inches, but it's enough to feel the difference. Then, for the first time since we've joined like this, he thrusts into me.

I shut my eyes but still see the light, just like a lunar eclipse where the moon moves into the sun's shadow. I had thought I was the sun. I now see I'm wrong. I'm only a moon shining in the light of his sun as the rays of his being fuck into me.

CHAPTER 19

VIRIUS

I can't breathe, which isn't exactly a problem, as vampires do not need to breathe to live. We only need to replenish the blood in our veins.

Zahara's blood courses through my body. Her essence zigs and zags like a bolt of thunder. It radiates outward as it treks down my throat. It arrows into my arms and legs, making my fingers and toes tingle. When it gets to my chest, it expands the chambers of my heart, making the organ feel as though it will burst.

It's not my heart that bursts from the joy of having her inside of me. It's my cock that is ready to explode from being inside her.

I can feel every pull of flesh. Every give of tendon. Every clench of muscle.

And so, I don't breathe. If I take one more breath, I will burst open. Not just my cock, my whole being.

Because she is the sun: the thing every vampire craves,

but can never touch for threat of death. Zahara will be the death of me.

I'm going to die because I can't keep my hands off her.

My heart is racing. Not because I'm exhausted or spent, but because blood circulates to reach every part of my body that demands more of her.

My mouth is dry. Not from physical hunger. I've drunk enough of her. But I want more. I need more. Not for sustenance, only for the pleasure of having her on my tongue.

My throat is thick. Not because I need air or food. Because there are words I want to say to her. But I'm not the poet in the family.

I wish Gaius was here. Although, if he was, if he saw my sun-filled kitten like this, I'd have to kill him. Then I'd never know what to say.

I held still while Zahara worked herself down and onto my length. She shudders and gasps as her orgasm takes her. The intimate massage of her muscles forces my eyes shut and once more, I see starlight. A million suns dance behind my eyelids. Zahara's sunlight penetrates not only my eyes but all of my skin. My bones. My very soul.

I'm certain I'm about to blow my load. It's the last thing I want to do. What I want to do is thrust into her—slowly, not the pounding beast I gave to the women who used me over all those years. To my surprise, my cock wants the same thing.

My balls relax... only a little. That tiny bit of retraction allows some give in my cockhead, and the swelling recedes... only a little. That small recession allows for more space in Zahara's channel, giving the length of my cock room to move... only a little.

Zahara is draped over my chest. Her head is tucked into my neck as she catches her breath. Shudders still wrack her spent form.

I move my hands down and cup the globes of her ass. When I lift her hips—only a little—her shoulders roll back. She doesn't lift her head, but her tight cunny grabs hold of my tip as though I'm a pacifier she's not ready to relinquish.

I have no plans to let this woman go. Not in this lifetime. I'll still be holding on to her in the next.

Slowly, carefully, I slide her down my length. The pleasure of it is exquisite and unexpected. I have never moved a woman onto my cock. I was usually chained to a wall or bed to give them a false sense of security. I was nothing but a beast to them, a tool to use.

Not so with Zahara. She wants me. And I—my dick, my fangs, my beating heart—all of the parts that make up who and what I am, they—we—I want her.

Zahara purrs against my neck as I fit her back into my lap. When she is flush against the base of my cock, her ass settled on my balls, I hear a click like a lock turning as we fit into the place where we were meant to join. Tiny pinpricks dot my back as she sinks her claws into me. I know there will be two moons decorating my shoulder blades when we're done. Those, too, are now a part of me.

I lift her again. Still slow. There is no urgency for me. We have all the time in the world. This is how I want to spend the rest of my days, with my cock snug inside this woman. Her arms around me. My hands cupping her ass as I make her scream.

As I pull her down back onto me, she throws her head back. Her eyes are closed. Ecstasy is written all over her face.

My chest puffs up to know that I did that. I put that look there. I'm giving her this satisfaction, this bliss.

For hundreds of years, I cursed my cock. Had I known what was in store for the two of us, I would have waited. I would have kept it under lock and key in a chastity belt until I met this woman. Remained the vestal virgin covered in pure white robes. And then I would have whipped it out and presented it to her on a sacrificial altar.

It's what she's done for me—except for the white robes. Zahara saved herself for me. She waited for me. And I let myself be defiled for centuries.

"I've fucked a lot of women."

Zahara's head wobbles as though I've punched her in the chin. Her eyes blink open to stare down at me.

"Most of the time, I didn't have a choice. Other times, I just let it happen because I didn't care. It didn't mean anything, because I couldn't feel it."

Her eyes flash before she blinks it away. But not before I see the panther lurking there. Not before I hear the low, threatening growl from somewhere deep in her throat.

"I feel everything with you."

To punctuate my statement, I dig my fingers into her ass and pull her snug to me. She groans low when I gain another half-inch inside her channel. I part her ass cheeks in an effort to spread her wider as I rock upward to gain the other half of that inch. Her muscles are already working themselves into a frenzy in preparation for the orgasm to come.

"I love you," I tell her before I lose her to her pleasure. "You are like sunlight to me; something I never thought I'd see again. Yet you shine down on me."

Her lips tremble. Her features crumple from the delirium of orgasmic bliss to something sad. At the corners of both her eyes, teardrops form.

"Am I hurting you?"

She doesn't answer.

I'm sure I've gone too far. I've pushed too deeply inside of her. She must be in pain.

But when I try to pull away, to pull my monster cock out of her, she clings. Zahara wraps her arms around me and buries her face in my neck at the same time as she wraps her thighs around me, locking her ankles at my lower back so that she cannot be separated from me at all.

I can feel the teardrops against my neck. They run down my chest. The tracks stop once they reach my heart.

Zahara presses herself against me. She tightens her thighs around my waist. She angles her hips until she is milking my cock with her tight sheath.

I answer her movements, using my hold on her ass to slide her up and down my cock. I can tell she wants to go fast. But the hell will I ever fuck this woman like those cunts from centuries ago. I want to feel every nook and cranny of Zahara. I want to know every part of her that she gives me access to.

Zahara's tears don't stop. They continue to fall as her orgasm takes her. With a gasp of pleasure, she finds my lips. She trembles in my arms, around my cock, as she cries into my mouth, sharing her bliss with me.

I grip her to me as my balls release the motherload. I empty everything that I am, everything that I was, and everything that I hope to be, inside her tight channel.

As I do, Zahara holds me tight, her arms, her legs, her body a sheath around me as I experience a bodily orgasm for the first time in my long life. And for the first time in my life, when I come down from the bone-shuddering pleasure, I am left feeling whole.

CHAPTER 20

ZAHARA

I watch Virius's chest as it rises and falls. Again, the movement is so slight that I find I'm holding my breath until his large pecs rise less than half an inch.

I've been like this all morning, barely blinking as I keep a vigil over his virility. His nostrils do not flare to bring in air. His lips do not sigh out upon exhale. Because he doesn't breathe.

Which means he doesn't snore. Which I guess is a plus. I have a lover who satisfied my body enough to knock me out, and is silent enough in sleep that I won't be rudely awakened in the afterglow. Instead of luxuriating in dreamland, I'm wide awake and watching for signs of life.

Intellectually, I know that he is a vampire and breathing is wholly unnecessary. It's his heartbeat that I'm watching. The organ keeps a slow and steady rhythm now that Virius's body is flush with my blood.

He is alive, though undead. He is strong, because of the

life essence that I gave him. But he will die because of the life essence he's destined to give to me.

I brush a blond curl from his forehead. Some of the eyelashes that touch his high cheekbones are the same pale shade—a forest of light and shadows that cover eyes that hide nothing.

For the few days that I've known him, Virius has hidden nothing from me. He has shared everything that he has to give. Even the one thing he feared would hurt me.

Frankie rests fitfully under the blanket that covers us. Even in its flaccid state, Virius's manhood is longer and thicker than the average man's. It still baffles me that all of him fits inside me. The soreness between my thighs reminds me that he did.

That soreness is a beautiful ache that I want to feel again. And then again. For the rest of my life.

An average-sized cock won't do. I'm not a size queen, as Virius called the women who abused him. It's not the size I care about. The old adage is true; size doesn't matter. It's how Virius uses his body that has me addicted.

Virius Serrano used his body to please me. To protect me. To love me.

I know that he found pleasure in me. Now I just need to find a way to protect him. Because my heart is telling me that I love this man.

His heartbeat speeds up, as though it just heard my silent declaration. I snatch my hand away from his chest.

He doesn't stir. He doesn't open his eyes. He doesn't reach for me—all of which makes it no easier for me to move away from him.

I climb out of the bed, but I can't tear my gaze away from him. His big body appears small in the bed. Vulnerable. He is the larger predator, but he's let a cat with claws into his home.

My fingers ball into fists. I feel sharp pricks against my palms as my nails dig into my own flesh. It takes everything in me to turn away from Virius, but I do.

I need to get out of here, but I'm naked. I could shift, but I feel too weary to make the transition. My panther has curled into a ball, as though she's mourning the loss of a mate. Panthers don't mate for life, but she doesn't seem to hear that. She sees Viri as hers.

Since I won't get out of here on four legs, I walk into Viri's closet on two. The clothing I find inside the walk-in curls my lip. It is a cosplayer's dream. Everything from breeches and waistcoats, to kaftans, to kilts, to a Zoot suit, to Armani.

I pull on a sari made of fine Indian silk, and pad out of the room.

It's late in the afternoon, by the position of the sun in the sky. A glance over at the clock in a sitting room confirms it. Outside a set of glass doors, the Serrano vineyards stretch as far as the eye can see.

This was once the land of my father's people: a small group of humans within the Tohono O'odham tribe who developed the ability to shift their shapes. But with a flourish of pen on parchment, the land was taken from them. Now, with a digital print out of documents, the land will be mine again.

That should thrill me. But it doesn't. Ownership of the land is only one aspect of the prophecy. The Serranos' signature on a deed can't stop what is coming.

Stepping outside, I take in a deep breath of the fresh air—and wince. There's a sickly sweet smell to the air. Like rotted fruit.

That is the other part of the prophecy. Long ago, my father's people angered the shifter god. He made it so that nothing would grow atop the soil until his anger was appeased. That would only happen when the Night Sun greeted the dawn. That night is tonight.

At the edge of the vineyard, I see movement. I go instantly into panic mode, thinking that it's someone from my tribe. But there are no red-headed jaguar shifters.

Marechal Durand is bent over a cluster of lush vines. I frown at the sight of my former employer, and the grapevine. The vineyard shouldn't be producing anything.

Marechal looks up with a grin when she sees me. "I think I've figured it out."

She holds one of the diseased vines in her hands. The white splotches along the roots and leaves cause me to wrinkle my sensitive nose. As a human, Marechal likely can't smell the decay that's killing the vines before they can bear fruit.

"I thought it was just root rot," she says, as though she's presenting findings to a committee. "But it goes deeper."

I want to say, *duh.* It does go deeper. It goes centuries deep, into a curse on my ancestors. Science won't cure this prophecy. Only a child born of a shifter and a vampire would break it. But I'm not going to bother to argue mystics with a degreed white woman.

To illustrate her scientific find, Marechal digs her hands into the soil. She places her sample in some kind of container and then holds it up to me as her evidence.

"Do you see?" she asks.

I don't.

"Too much fertilizer."

I might not know how to read the chemical symbols on the device, but I know what that means. Too much fertilizer in the soil can make vines grow leaves, but no fruit.

"There's too much nitrogen in the fertilizer," she continues. "It's as though the nitrogen is making the soil too dark for the plants to see the light. We just need to add phosphorous to help absorb the light. Then these little mamas will bear fruit next season."

Marechal turns back to her work. She takes another vial of chemicals out of the case. The label has a big P in black, covering the glass tube. Marechal pours some of the powder into the mixture. It bubbles and fizzes like a witch's brew.

I stand behind her. My legs can't move. My chest feels constricted. My fingertips tingle.

After a few moments, Marechal's face lights up. "See?"

I see that a reaction has happened, but I'm not sure what it is.

"It just needed balance," she continues. "This land has been untouched and left in the dark for years. All it needed was a little help to see the light."

"Are you saying the grapes will grow now?" I ask.

"Give me nine months, and I'll have this place bearing fruit."

Marechal grins brightly at her scientific achievement. I stand mute, questioning my very reason for being.

Gaius, Hadrian and Virius all said that prophecies never turn out as expected. Those three vampires are just as old as this curse. And all the parts of it are coming undone and being righted in unexpected ways.

If the land is now mine because of a pen stroke, and the grapes will grow and bear fruit because of chemistry... then maybe the prophecy is satisfied? Maybe... maybe it's even wrong?

Maybe I don't have to get pregnant?

Maybe I can keep Virius forever?

CHAPTER 21

VIRIUS

I struggle to awaken. Not because I'm tied down, not this evening. There are no binds that hold me to the bed as I wait to be petted by Domitia's newest client. My hands and legs are free. My body is my own. It's only the setting sun that weighs me down.

Still, I rise in defiance of the life-threatening rays. It's the first time I can remember waking up with a light, airy halo around my head. The first time that warmth courses through my chest. I think this is called happiness.

Though, when I turn in the bed, the source of my happiness is not with me.

I should panic. But I don't. I scent her nearby. She hasn't gone far. Even if she had, I would track her down.

Domitia bound me to her with her blood, with chains, and with words that mindfucked a child into submission. It wasn't until last night that I finally shook off the last vestiges of that bondage. Now, I'm bound to Zahara. But this time, I've cuffed myself.

I will gladly spend the rest of my life giving Zahara pleasure, fulfilling her every need and desire. Including giving her the child she desires.

It's a trudge to get out of the bed. There's likely a half hour of sunlight left outside. Inside my closet, I feel for the first garment on a hanger. I poke the correct body parts through the appropriate holes, and go in search of my woman.

Her scent trail leads me to the back of the house. A few rays of sunlight shine in from the glass doors that lead out to the vineyard. I step my way around those shards of death until I am on one side of the window.

Zahara sits in a cluster of vines. Her legs are folded beneath her. In her hands, she holds a diseased vine. Marechal is beside her. Scientific instruments are all around them.

I can hear what they're saying thanks to my supernatural hearing. But they're speaking in the unintelligible language of science, so their words go over my head. I don't bother to catch any of the discussion. I simply let the tone of Zahara's voice wash over me.

Even her voice is like honey as it enters my ears—which makes sense, since her kisses are like nectar. Between her thighs it tastes like the sweetest of wines. Her blood would shame the ambrosia of the gods.

The need to have her in my arms, her thighs wrapped around my neck, around my waist, is so powerful that I take a step towards the door. I hiss as the light shoves me back into the shadows.

"Just a few more minutes, and then we can go to them."

I don't turn at the sound of Gaius's voice. I sense him behind me, and am sure his gaze is on Marechal.

"Crazy what love does," Gaius continues. "It fills you with such want that it makes you forget your weaknesses."

"Have you learned any more about how Dom fathered a child?"

Gaius's pause lets me know that he has.

"Tell me," I demand.

"I don't know the answer. But I know where we can find Dom."

"Let's go," I say, eager to learn how to give Zahara the one thing I never thought I could.

"In a minute."

Gaius reaches for the door and pulls it open. The sun has set, thus lifting the barrier between the two of us and the women we treasure. Gaius is on Marechal in less than a breath. Both she and Zahara yelp at his sudden appearance.

Marechal giggles as Gaius brings her up into his arms for a deep and bruising kiss. Zahara blinks at the two of them. Then, as though only just sensing my presence, she turns to me.

I'm not certain what to do. Should I race to her? Bring her into my arms, and kiss her? That's what I want to do. But I'm uncertain if I should.

Hadrian made Cari a vampire and bound her to him in our ways. Gaius plans to do the same with Marechal, in time. I know that Zahara is mine, but I don't know how panther shifters mate. Wolves bite. I've already bitten her. That should stake my claim.

The thoughts flee my mind as a bundle of flesh is flung into my arms. Zahara removes all my doubts as she wraps her legs and arms around me and presses her mouth against mine.

"You're awake," she says against my lips.

"I would never sleep if I could touch you all day." I lick at her bottom lip, then graze the top one with my fang, marveling that I have the right to do so.

"Let's go back to your room so you can touch me all night."

She is beautiful in the blood-red of the moonlight. That's when I note the color of the night. It's the night of the lunar eclipse. The moon is in the shadow of the sun. Some of the sun's light passes through the satellite, but the dilution isn't enough to burn a vampire.

"There's something I must do first," I tell her.

Zahara's grin turns down into a frown. "Are we back to you turning down sex again?"

I press a kiss to her frown. "I won't be long."

"You forget that you're my captive," she says as she tightens her arms and legs around me. "You're supposed to do as you're told."

I grip her ass in my hands. My cock is ready to follow her command. To let her know that her request was heard, I press her core up against the evidence. Her gaze immediately goes hooded.

"I promise I won't be long," I repeat. "Then I'll let you boss me around."

"You'll let—"

I capture her lips in another kiss. When she gasps, I invade her mouth. My tongue tangles with hers as though in a duel. If we had more time, I'd let her win. I'd let her have a taste of the control she thinks she wants. But I need to make this quick, and get the answers I need to give her what she truly wants: a child.

So, I suck at her tongue until she mewls. When she gives, I score the tip of her tongue with a fang. I pull at the droplet of her blood that pools there. It's only an appetizer. I'll be back for the main course as soon as possible.

When I set Zahara down, she wobbles. She clings to me,

and I can see stars in her dazed eyes. I hold her until she regains her balance.

"Fine," she says clearing her throat. "You can go. But don't be long."

"As you command," I say, stealing another taste of her before I head off with Gaius.

I plan to follow that last order. I plan to learn how to give her the child she wants. Then she'll have everything she asked for. And it will be me who gave it to her, and not some fool prophecy.

CHAPTER 22

VIRIUS

I press my fingers to my lips. The pressure of my fingertip causes a dam at the center of my bottom lip. On either side the blood backs up, waiting impatiently to rush into the divot.

Slipping my tongue beneath my finger, I lick at the skin there. I can still taste her on my lips. She's at the corners of my mouth as well. She is under my tongue. Her honey fills my throat.

Zahara is all around me. She is inside me. She is my entire world now. And I will give her everything she has ever dreamed of.

"We're here."

Gaius puts the car in park outside a club in downtown Tucson. The place doesn't share the same upscale class that clings to the velvet ropes of Club Toxic. But its dark decor still beckons those who seek the nightlife.

Inside, the layout is that of an actual club and not a

BDSM cover. A bar sits in one corner. Tables and chairs dot the walls. The focal point of the room is the stage where musical instruments lie in wait for their masters.

A woman is on the stage. She runs her hands over each instrument. She doesn't strum chords or strike keys, but there is a hum coming from the stage, as though the music is eager to get out of her.

"Mama, listen."

Clanging and thumps ring out from the stage as a child bangs and thrashes the drum set. Surprisingly, the raucous is rhythmic and systematic. The child's playing sounds like what could be called music.

"You got it, baby. Rock on, Luci." The woman bobs her head in time to the music. Maternal pride is stretched wide on her face as she smiles at the kid.

"We're closed," says a male voice that carries as much bass as the drum set. "Show starts at ten."

"We're not here for the show," says Gaius, his trademark smile in place. "My brother and I are here to talk to you."

This must be Dom, I think, though I frown as I look at the man. He doesn't smell like a vampire. Not exactly. He doesn't entirely smell human, though I can scent the blood rushing through him. I hear it pumping through his heart.

The harsh breath of air he pushes through his teeth seems like a loss of more than his temper. Dom inhales, as though he needs the breath to make words come out of his frowning mouth. "Whatever it is, I'm not interested."

"What are you?" I say.

Dom turns his gaze on me. He might not be a full vampire anymore, but he is still a dangerous male. "I'm the man who's about to throw you out of here on your ass if you don't get your fangs away from my family."

I glance back at the stage. The beating of the drums has gone silent. The woman stands in front of the child. Her hands are balled into fists as though she will tear through us if we take a step towards them.

"He's yours?" I say, looking at the kid holding the drumsticks. "How did you do that?"

"If you're looking for the Sex Ed class," says the child's mother, "go across town to the middle school."

"Mama, what's sex ed?" says the kid.

Both parents wince at the inquiry.

"Kate, take him to the back, will you?" says Dom.

Kate wrinkles her features behind Dom's back. She digs in her heels as though she's reluctant to leave him alone with two vampires who could easily tear her and her child apart for a light meal.

"Now." Dom doesn't raise his voice. He also doesn't put any extra bass in the command. But it is unmistakably a command.

Instead of bristling at the order, a slight shiver shimmies across Kate's shoulders. It's the universal language of a submissive lowering her head to her Dominant's will.

"Come on, Luci. Daddy's got company to deal with."

Kate and Luci walk off the stage and head to the back. My gaze trails them. My heart pounds hard in my chest as I watch them go. That could be Zahara in a few years. I just need to find out how Dom did it.

"I need a child," I say.

Dom growls, sounding more like a lion than a man who is no longer a vampire.

"Not your child. I need a spawn of my own loins."

I point to my crotch area. Dom does not look down. He doesn't take his eyes off me. His body remains between me and Gaius, and the path his family took.

The protective instinct fascinates me. I never knew my father. Every man I came in contact with wanted to either use his fists or his cock to hurt me—every man other than Gaius and Hadrian.

Dom looks like he'd use his fist to rip my cock off and shove it down my throat if I dared take a step towards his mate or his child. A fire starts in my gut that tells me that I would do the same if anyone dared harm Zahara and her child.

No, *our* child.

I have never truly given any thought to having a child. Not even when I was human. I would never want to produce a living being who was born into bondage like I was.

Zahara thinks our child will be born with a job to do: to break a curse. But that would only be a belief. I've already given my land, my money, and my heart to Zahara. Our child would be born free to do whatever they wanted.

Born free. Made with love. That is something I'd like to create.

"How?" I ask Dom.

His gaze rakes over me. His stance doesn't relax, but his lips start moving. "It's a bloody business."

I shrug. My life has been nothing but blood and pain.

"I was drained by a vampire called Roxanna," Dom goes on. "She wanted to make me her minion, to do her bidding without a thought. She almost did."

"She must have known our sire, Domitia," says Gaius. "We were nothing but her pets when she wanted to play. Her executioners when she was hungry and bored. We broke free of her, but not without loss."

"Same here," says Dom.

"But you are no longer a vampire," I say. "You smell mortal."

"I am," says Dom. "Mostly."

"How?" I ask.

"Kate," he says simply. "I was near death after Roxanna

drained me. Kate told me to connect with the spiritual sun. She insisted that my true essence would remain, that it was stronger than Roxanna's will. Kate was right. When I came out of it, my mortality was restored. So, I age."

Dom lifts his hand to indicate the gray streaks in his hair.

"What mortality I gained gave me just enough to create a new life and live out my days alongside my love."

"Is that all?" I ask.

I had expected a gauntlet filled with quests and challenges, and lots of blood and pain. But it appears that the way to regain my mortality is the same way I lost it: be drained of blood. But instead of being fed the blood of a vampire, I need to cling to a soul I'm not sure I have. That will be the tricky part.

"Is that all!" Gaius turns to me, his face contorted in anger and disbelief. "That's enough. It sounds like you could die."

If that's the cost to give Zahara what she wants, I will pay it. If I can make a new life that is born free, that is the legacy I want to leave to this world. It would make all the misery and pain of my long life worth it.

CHAPTER 23

ZAHARA

"Now that you're rich, what's the first thing you're going to buy?" asks Carignan Durand.

Cari, Marechal, and I sit in the formal dining room. A spread of gourmet food is displayed across the table. Cari sips blood from a glass chalice. Marechal slices into frog legs in a buttery sauce then washes the reptilian fare down with a glass of wine whose cost would feed a small village.

I hold a silver spoon in my hand as I chew on *Boeuf Bourguignon*, which is rich people speak for beef stew. It has all the hallmarks of *hilachas*, a Guatemalan beef stew with tomatillo sauce. Except the tomatoes taste like spring in the fall time. The onions kick back. The spices hit my nose as if I'm pulling them straight from the ground.

Yeah, there really is a difference between how the wealthy and the rest of us live. And it's being proven here at the dinner table. But I still don't feel like I'm rich. I'm still wearing a borrowed dress, no shoes, and no underwear.

"It's not like she needs anything," says Marechal, sliding a small bit of meat into her mouth and then setting her fork and knife down as though she's done.

I'm not judging, because I've eaten frogs before. But it was while I was in panther form. The creatures couldn't even be called an appetizer, they were so small. I have no idea how she's had enough. I'm on my second bowl of *bourguignon,* and eyeing the pot for a third helping.

"True," says Cari, licking the blood from her upper lip. "She now owns this house, the land. I think Viri has a couple of cars in the garage. He'll likely have a personal shopper deliver a full wardrobe in the morning. Hadrian did that the first night we spent together."

"I don't need any of that," I say, finally able to get a word in edgewise with the Durand sisters. For the last hour, they've been talking around me as though I wasn't even there. But I probably have some fault in that. I worked for the Durands for years and was used to holding my tongue when my bosses spoke. But now I'm the boss.

"What do you want to do?" Cari sets her glass down. "Travel?"

I inhale as I think about it. The idea of traveling to places beyond the southern border of North America is an intriguing one. But it isn't an immediate need. And it isn't one I could have fulfilled any time soon.

There is still the nagging noose of the prophecy wrapped tight around my belly. I press my hand there now. The beef is going down well, but my stomach grumbles. It wants to be full, but not with life. It wants to be full with something else entirely.

"I want to go to school."

There is silence after I speak the words. I shut my mouth, wishing I could take them back. I have never said them out loud before. But now, they're out there. I cringe as I wait for the laughter to fill the ornate dining area.

"That's so cool," says Cari. "I was thinking of going back to school, too."

"Where have you applied?" asks Marechal. "The University of Arizona is an excellent school."

"I was going to get a history degree," says Cari. "Specializing in the Dark Ages and the Renaissance, so that I can learn more about my husband's past."

"We have a relationship with the University of Phoenix," says Marechal. "We donated a garden. So, if you need a recommendation..."

I look between the two women. There is no mirth on their faces. There is no frown of disapproval. No reminder of the duty I'm destined to fulfill. There's only acceptance.

Oh, to be a rich white woman who thinks the world will simply bend its will to meet her needs.

But I'm not a rich white woman.

I'm a rich indigenous woman who now has the means to bend the world to her needs. Or had I forgotten?

The land of my ancestors has been returned to me. The vineyard will yield fruit in a year's time. The man who was meant to be the father of my child wants to spend the rest of his life with me.

I kinda have it all. There's nothing stopping me from going to college if that's what I want. There's nothing forcing me to have a child right now if that's not what I want.

I look out the window at the dark night. The moon has begun its process of moving in front of the sun. It's already casting a warm glow, heralding the commencement of a prophecy that has already been fulfilled.

Destiny always finds you? But I got here ahead of it. I've already passed the test and turned it in before the time was up. Shouldn't that get me extra credit? Shouldn't it at least get me out of the final exam?

"Let me know where you decide to go," says Cari. "Then I'll apply there too. We can be coeds together. But it'll have to be after I get my fangs under control."

Cari touches her index finger to one of her incisors. The sharp point pricks the flesh of her fingertip. A dot of blood escapes, which she promptly sucks away.

"I'm doing really well," she says with a grin. "I haven't bitten you, and your blood smells absolutely divine."

Cari inhales, her nostrils flaring. Her eyelids close and her long lashes touch down against her high cheekbones. She lets out a moan that sounds like a purr.

Before I can go on the defensive, Virius appears in the doorway. Cari clears her throat and throws back the last of the blood in her wine glass. But I've already forgotten about the baby vampire.

Virius darkens the door, but there's a smile on his face. A look of absolute joy. I've risen and am in his arms before I realize I've moved.

I meant to ask him where he's been, what he was up to, what happened to bring that smile to his face when it didn't originate with him between my thighs. But the taste of his grin is so intoxicating that I find myself licking and sucking at his lips instead of making words.

Virius returns my kiss with vigor, with joy, with complete abandon. It takes a moment before I hear the throat clearing behind us. I open my eyes, but do not take my lips from Virius's mouth.

Gaius is looking down at us with complete and utter disapproval. I want to tell him that I have more class than to strip down and do it in the dining room. But there's a part of me, the part that splits my thighs into a V, that would beg to differ.

"Did you know about this?" Gaius asks.

I have no idea what he's talking about. In order to answer, I'll need to take my mouth from Viri's. I do so reluctantly. "Know about what?"

"In order to break the curse, he needs to die."

All the blood drains from my person. It goes so fast that my heart skips a few beats. When I look at Virius, he doesn't look angry. He wears the same open acceptance and wonder that he first regarded me with.

I know two things for sure at this moment. I know that Virius would die for me if I asked it of him. More importantly, I know that I will never ask it of him, even if it means others will suffer.

The reason why is simple; I love this man.

CHAPTER 24

VIRIUS

The flare of Zahara's nostrils confuses me. The deep crease that settles low into her brow baffles me. The lowering of her hooded gaze disorients me.

If I were to put all of those facial expressions together, it would lead me to believe that my mate is angry. But that can't be right. I'm giving her everything her heart desires: the land, the money, even the impossible child.

But then I look again. When I do, I see I missed a key feature that led me to the wrong conclusion.

On Zahara's cheeks, there is a deep red burn where the blood has pooled. That expression is one I know all too well. It is the look of shame.

Reaching out, I cup her face in one of my hands. Her skin is hot to my touch. Her eyes close like a loud door slamming in my face.

"You do not want my child?" I say. It is the only thing that makes sense.

Zahara's eyelids rise high. Her feline gaze flashes at me. That blinding light from the animal inside her shows not a hint of shame. That is definitely anger. "I don't want you to die."

"Oh." I smile, pleased at the vehemence in her tone at the potential of my demise. "It's not an actual death. I would simply lose my immortality."

Behind me, I hear Gaius grinding his molars. I know Hadrian has come into the room as well. He doesn't gasp his shock, but he vibrates with tension.

I can't spare my brothers any of my attention. My gaze never wavers from Zahara. She is the center of my universe.

I watch as the sunlight within her continues to wax and wane. Clouds move across her gaze as though a storm is only moments away. This storm won't be a light spring sprinkle. This promises the torrential rains of a hurricane.

"What is he talking about?" says Hadrian.

"We went to see Dom," Gaius answers. "Apparently, the vampirism can be reversed."

"How?" says Marechal.

From the corner of my eyes, I see Marechal go into Gaius's arms. Gaius's arms move slowly around her. But once he has Marechal in his embrace, it's as though the lead has left his body and he radiates warmth around her.

The same happens when Cari goes to Hadrian.

"Dom, another vampire, was bled dry," Gaius says. "He survived by reconnecting with his soul, or the light, or some such woo-woo nonsense. I don't know. But his mortality was restored."

"Bleeding?" says Zahara. "No one said anything about bleeding."

"So you did know," Gaius accuses her.

"I knew…" Zahara clears her throat and closes her eyes. When she tries to raise her gaze, it falters. When she tries her voice again, it is only a whisper. "The prophecy indicates that he would die before the child is born."

She raises her gaze now. The sorrow in her eyes nearly knocks me down. A tear pools at the corner of her eye. I catch it before it can fall.

Another joins the first. And then another. I cradle Zahara's face in my hands and let the tears fall.

"I'm sorry," she says.

"I will not die," I say, leaning my forehead against hers. "I've been dead all my life. The first time I ever felt alive is the moment I met you."

Zahara presses her lips together. She looks as though she's struggling to let words out. Or keep them in. I'm not sure which.

"You are my destiny, Zahara. If I was born simply to spend a few days loving you and then die giving you a child, that time will be a life well-lived."

"No," she says, the single word a forceful gale against my lips. "I do not want this destiny. I do not want this child. I just want you."

"You have me."

"And I'm keeping you. You are mine. Mine."

I cannot stop the grin that spreads across my face. This wee little kitten was right. I am her captive. I will happily bind myself to her for the rest of my days, however many they are.

"You gave me the land. Marechal figured out what's wrong with the vines. As far as I'm concerned, this prophecy is fulfilled."

"But the child?" I say.

"I don't want a child."

I wince at the vehemence in those words. It's clear she means it. The little cherub I've been dreaming of since the car ride home, the little boy with her dark hair and my light eyes—in my mind, I see him crying at his mother's rejection. I see him shoved out of the room as his mother takes another male to bed. I see him sitting on the street, begging for a crumb of bread because there is no one in the world who cares about him.

"I want this child," I say.

In my mind's eye, the little boy looks up. Something sparkles in his eyes. It's faint, but it's there. It's a small light of hope.

"Well, you're not putting it in my womb."

Zahara lifts her chin in that defiant pose that made me hard just hours ago. For the first time, I do not stir below. She steps towards me, shoving a claw-tipped finger into my chest. The point of it is a dagger in my heart.

"And if you dare think of sticking Frankie into any other woman—"

"Who's Frankie?"

"—I'll claw her eyes out. Her tits, too."

Zahara turns on her heel and heads to the glass door of the patio. I take a step to follow, but she growls at me.

It's not a low warning growl. It's a growl of pure menace. One that says: *fuck with me and I'll take a bite out of you.*

By the Fates, I love this woman.

Zahara opens the door and steps out. She reaches down and lifts the hem of her sundress up and over her head. I want to growl at my brothers to avert their gazes from her nakedness. But I am left speechless as her body begins to transform.

The smooth skin I love to kiss grows dark fur. The heart-shaped mouth that leaves me drunk, elongates into a muzzle. The tall, proud woman goes down to all fours as she shifts fully into a black panther.

She is magnificent. She is beautiful. She is mine, and our children will be perfect.

As though she can hear my thoughts, my panther growls at me again. This time, she flashes teeth. I have half a mind to challenge her to a fight, just so that I can tackle her to the ground and show her that I will not be budged from my position.

But I know my little warrior. She needs to believe that she is in control of this situation. So I drop my gaze as though in submission, and allow her a head start before I chase after her.

CHAPTER 25

ZAHARA

y stomach turns in knots as I run through the vineyard. Even though I've just eaten two helpings of the fancy beef stew, my stomach feels empty. That's why it's grumbling and hissing as my paws strike the ground. That is the ache that needs to be filled.

The moon's light shines down upon me. Its rays feel warm tonight, like the light of the sun. I shrug off the light for the shadows.

I don't want to be anyone's light. I want the darkness around me. If the prophecy can't find me, if it can't see me, then it won't happen.

So what if the thought is childish? I've been treated like a child all my life. Every decision has been made for me by those who thought they knew better. Well, they'll just have to deal with this tantrum because I am about to raise hell in the middle of the mall. Too bad I'm alone in a vineyard.

I scent the prey at the far edge of the vineyard. Deer are typically a nuisance for the foliage that grows on the vineyards. Too bad this deer decided to come in for a late-night snack when a pissed off panther was on the prowl.

I move silently towards it. The creature is yards away from me. It doesn't scent me yet, but it does sense me.

Its ears twitch. Its mouth pauses in chewing the leaves it's stolen. My leaves. This is my land.

As though my anger is a living, breathing thing, the deer appears to sense it. I stay in place, holding still. Unlike other predators like wolves, my kind doesn't chase their prey until they tire. I wait until the deer is within range, and then I pounce.

I leap into the air, springing nearly fifteen feet to close in on the kill. My claws extend. My front paws grasp around the animal's shoulders. I'm preparing to rip out its neck when I notice an unexpected scent. The sweet scent of mother's milk.

I have a doe in my clutches. She has milk in her breasts. Somewhere nearby, there is likely a gangly-legged Bambi watching this murder go down.

I retract my claws and let the doe go. She hobbles off into the night. The trail of her blood might make it easy for another predator to track her down.

There's nothing I can do about that. She had been set in my path. If it's her destiny to die tonight, then I can't stop it.

What I can do is stop the death of the man I love. Whether he likes it or not. There will be no Bambi for us. Despite what he thinks, despite what everyone thinks, there's no need.

The prophecy has proven it doesn't need to be followed to the letter. The land was restored to its rightful owners without any bloodshed.

Well, technically Viri did bite me. But I allowed it. Hell, I want him to sink his fangs into me again, and soon.

The berries will produce. That's all thanks to science and not magic. Which has to mean that my loins don't need to bear any fruit. Which has to mean that Virius doesn't have to die.

At the entrance to the caves, I shift. I walk into the underground clearing on two human legs. On the walls hang robes in white and light blue—the colors of Guatemala, where many of these women are from. Those original descendants of the Tohono O'odham who went down south from our ancestral lands dress in jeans and blouses instead of the manatees and moccasins of the old days.

I pull a sheath over my head as I proceed deeper into the belly of the cave. The women are gathered in clusters. I note that the clusters don't resemble the two factions of days ago. Itzel and Zuma have their heads bowed together as they speak in hushed voices.

When I look closer, I see that they are standing around a raised altar. A large, drab, gray stone decorates the dais. Four sets of chains and manacles hang from each corner.

"What the actual fuck?"

All gazes turn to me. Only a few of those pairs of eyes then cast downward in shame.

Itzel's flash in exasperation. "Where is he?"

"Is that for him?" I demand, ignoring her question. "Is that for me too? Did you expect us to do it out in the open for all of you to watch? What the hell do you think this is? Some *Eyes Wide Shut* crap?"

Itzel stares at me mutely. I should have known she wouldn't know the erotic film about rich white people. Itzel feels that all media is twisted history. Zuma, on the other hand, smirks at the reference.

"Where is the Night Son, Ixazaluoh?"

"He's not coming."

Itzel sighs. Once upon a time, her disappointment would snap my butt into action. Not tonight.

"I won't let him die," I say.

"You cannot escape destiny."

"Destiny can go to the devil. I've already fixed everything." I step up to the dais, making sure to avoid the chains so that everyone can see and hear me. "Viri signed over the land to me. It's ours again. Marechal Durand figured out what's wrong with the vines. The soil just needed the right fertilizer. So you see, everything has worked out. We got everything that we wanted."

A low murmur goes through the gathered women. The hum sounds hesitant, uncertain. I don't blame them. We've all been on this path for decades, but now it's over. We can all stop this quest, and start to live our lives.

I can live my life. With Viri. While going to school and becoming… whatever I want to be.

"That does not fulfill the prophecy," says Itzel. "The gods demand the child."

"Well, I don't want to get pregnant. And you can't make me."

My womb is my own. My body is my own. The only thing I'm willing to give up is my heart. It's back on the surface with Virius, who I know is coming for me. I'm surprised he let me get this far without giving chase.

"It's not up to you, child," says Itzel.

"I'm not a child," I hiss.

Itzel reaches her hand up to my face and cups my cheek. A shiver goes through my spine at her touch. How had I not noticed before how leathery her fingers feel? How had I not noticed before the frown lines in her lips?

I don't get a chance to think over any of that now. A sharp pain explodes at the back of my head. I have just enough time to see Pia over my shoulder. She shrugs apologetically as I begin to slump. The last thing I see is the rock in her hand. The last thing I think is to pray to the gods that Virius stays away. But in my heart, I know he won't.

CHAPTER 26

VIRIUS

"You're not going after her."

I look down at the hand clasping my arm. Gaius's fingers are elegant, though I know the excruciating torture they are capable of. For years, I watched him bind and thrash humans to within an inch of their lives before drinking from them, or executing them during the Inquisition. I stood right alongside him, doing the same work. Though my fingers still appear stained with blood.

"It could be the end of you if you go through with this," says Gaius.

I am touched that he cares. Only he and Hadrian have ever cared for me. For centuries, I have been a satellite in their orbits. Zahara is my sun.

"I have to," I say. "She is my destiny."

Hadrian steps up to the other side of me, boxing me in. "Please, brother. Let's just take a moment to think this through."

Instead of fighting either of them, I wrap an arm around Hadrian's shoulder. With the other, I embrace Gaius. The two men hold me tight, as though they won't let me go. But I know the words to loosen their hold on me.

"If Carignan or Marechal asked this of you, would you not find a way?"

I miscalculated. The bonds my brothers had around me increase as Cari and Marechal join in the group hug. The two women have never touched me before. I can't blame them, as my abuse always made me leery of women.

But this affection from them, I understand. They are my family. Like Gaius and Hadrian, they aren't going to let me go without a fight.

"I'm going to go after her," I say inside the cocoon. "She and I will talk about this matter between ourselves. And then we'll fill you in on our decision."

There is some reluctance. But slowly, each man and woman begins to loosen their hold. Gaius is the holdout.

"Be home before dawn," he says. "If not, I'm coming after you with my belt." He says the words with a sardonic grin, so I know that on some level, he means it.

"Yes, Dad." I grin.

He cups my chin and gives me a fierce look. I turn from him, and I'm gone. Out the door and on my panther's trail.

I figured she would head back to the caves, back to her own family. But her scent is strong in the vineyard. I see her tracks in the soil, along with a deer's. So my kitten decided to take her anger out in a hunt.

Following the signs of the hunt, it's clear that Zahara overtook the deer. There is a clear sign of struggle in a clearing. However, the deer's tracks go off in one direction. Zahara's take a turn in the opposite direction.

So, she changed her mind? Perhaps that means that her anger has abated. A good sign for me.

I follow her tracks, which lead me to the cave entrance. For the second time in less than a week, I enter this place of my own free will. The first time had been to rescue Gaius from these shifters. Along the way, I had scented Zahara's sweet heat. When I came face to face with her, I knew that she was mine.

I scent that same heat now. She is here, amongst these women, in the sea of long dark hair and honey-brown skin. But I don't see her.

"Aren't you the valiant little knight, come to save the Indian princess," says a croaking voice.

My heart stops when my gaze lands on the white-haired woman. Her smile is proprietary, as if she owns me. Her gaze is calculating, as though she weighs my worth. I am a poor boy begging on the streets of Rome again, and Domitia has come for me.

But this isn't Rome, it's Arizona.

I'm not on the streets. This is a cave.

And this woman isn't Domitia. It's Zahara's kin: Itzel.

"You know this won't be one of those mouse movies where the white man subdues the natives and takes the princess?" says Itzel.

"Mouse movies?" I ask.

"She means Disney," says another woman. She is the cougar I saw arguing with Itzel days ago.

The cougar eyes me in the proprietary way of the women Domitia would hire to use me. I have the urge to cover myself as the cougar's gaze travels lower. Instead, I straighten to my full height in the cramped cave. She might look, but I will only ever touch Zahara.

"Excuse me." I snap my fingers. "My eyes are up here."

The cougar's face breaks into a grin. "I like him."

"Too bad," says Itzel. "He's only good for one purpose."

"I've come for Zahara," I say, not wishing to be a part of

this conversation any longer. I've said all I need to say to these two, and used up all the good manners Gaius taught me.

"That you certainly will do," says the cougar.

"Zahara will be with us in a moment," says Itzel.

She circles around to my back. I feel I should keep an eye on her. But she's a small woman. There's no physical damage she could do to me. But she could make things difficult between me and Zahara.

"Come, have a seat." Itzel points to a raised slab of stone.

My feet hesitate after I've taken the first step towards it. The slab reminds me of the dungeons in one of Domitia's castles. She liked to chain me up in the basement for the use of her clients. I could easily have broken the chains, but it was the psychological enslavement that Domitia got off on. And the chains made the wealthy women who sought my favor feel that they held all the power.

"I'll just go to her room," I say, taking a step away from the stone altar.

A sharp pain rakes across the back of my head. I look over to see that the cougar has struck me with a rock. She struck me hard, because I can see blood staining on the rock's surface.

The blow dazes me, but it doesn't bring me down. What does bring me down is the dagger to the chest. Itzel is on me as I fall to the ground. In the space of one moment, I have three thoughts.

My first thought is not to crush the old woman who is Zahara's relative.

My second thought is how unlike Zahara this woman looks and feels.

"Now you'll bleed." Itzel's voice sounds far away. "And when you're close to death, you will give us the child, and the gods will be appeased."

Bleed? Child? Gods?

My last thought is: why? I would have given Zahara this. I would have given her my life if it meant she would have the child she wanted. She didn't need to take it.

But what had I expected? I was born a slave. As I'm dragged to the altar and my wrists are shackled in chains, I know the answer to my last question: it's fitting that this is the way I'll die. It's exactly as I've lived my life. In bondage.

CHAPTER 27

ZAHARA

"*W*ake up, Zahara."

Everything aches. My head. My arms. My legs. Even my eyelids. So, naturally, opening my eyes is the last thing I want to do.

"Zahara, you have to wake up."

I slap at the hand shoving my shoulder. My fingers come away wet. When I open my eyes, I see blood on my claw tips.

I'm halfway through a shift. My panther feels like it's trying to leash the human part of me that wouldn't wake.

Pia stands over me, cradling her forearm. Blood seeps through her fingers. Her mouth is pursed, as though she's holding in her canines.

The word *sorry* doesn't enter my brain. The last thing I remember about Pia is the blow to the head she dealt me. I growl at her, preparing to give my body over to the panther to exact revenge for that cheap shot.

"Hey," she says, holding up her bloody hands. "We can

settle that score now. Or, you can deal with the more important matter at hand."

The only matter at hand is whooping the ass of this traitor and then getting the hell out of here to find Virius.

"The ritual has begun."

I blink a few times. Ritual? "It can't start unless…"

I can't bring myself to complete the sentence out loud. The ritual can't start unless Virius is here. Which means he's here.

Of course he's here. I knew he would follow me. In trying to get away from him, in trying to save his life, I led him right into the trap that would kill him.

"We have to hurry," says Pia.

"We?"

"If I hadn't taken you out, Itzel would've likely chained you to the altar to wait for him. Then you'd be helpless beside him."

I know time is of the essence, but I have to ask. "Why are you doing this? You tried to let Virius escape that first day. And now this. Why?"

"This isn't the way," says Pia. "I'm all for preserving our history and ways, but this? The virginal sacrifice and lambs to the slaughter bullshit, that needs to stay buried in the past."

"Right!" I agree.

Pia and I stand there in a moment of new age, feminist solidarity. Instead of doing a fist bump, I grab the handle of the door. I still have to get out there and rescue my man like the modern heroine that I am.

We turn out of the room and walk on silent feet down the narrow corridor. My palm presses against the cold, hard stone of the walls. My ears strain for any sign of Virius. I don't hear his deep baritone, but I do smell his unmistakable scent.

143

"He's not looking so good," says Zuma's voice.

Peering into the clearing, I see Zuma standing over the slab. Lying prone on his back is Virius. His eyes are closed. His sun-kissed skin looks pale. His large body looks sunken in.

"Maybe you should back off a bit there, Itzel. We don't want him to die."

"That is his destiny." Itzel tips a bucket on the floor towards her.

I see red. The red of Virius's blood drips from a wound in his wrists into the bucket. That isn't his only wound. There's a stake in his chest. They put a fucking stake into his chest.

I'm preparing to charge forth, but something holds me back. Pia.

It takes everything in me not to lash out at her. Looking into her eyes, I see what she's trying to say. We need a plan. There are twenty shifters watching the events unfold on that dais.

Some wear stoic, unfeeling faces. Most of the gazes are averted from the scene, as though they can't stomach the ritual either. But the stoic faces still outnumber the two of us who are ready to spring into action.

"Um, I know it's been a long time since you've gotten any," Zuma is saying. "But cocks don't stand up if the john they're attached to can't."

"The gods demand a sacrifice," says Itzel, pressing the wound on Virius's chest.

The blood flow from there has stopped. Oh Fates, is he already dead? Am I too late?

"Yeah, a sacrifice," says Zuma. "That's why he's chained to the altar. But he still needs to perform to get Zahara knocked up. Hell, with what he's carrying in his pants, he could knock us all up with one blow."

Zuma's fingers lift the waistband of Viri's pants. That is

the last straw for me. Hell no is that bitch eying my man's package.

I break free of Pia's hold, no longer willing to think over my next steps. I am pure rage and aggression. But before I can get to Itzel or Zuma, the entire cave shakes.

Rocks rain down over everyone gathered inside. Three figures appear at the cave's entrance. With the shifters' gazes focused on the newcomers, I make my way to Viri on the altar.

CHAPTER 28

VIRIUS

The darkness all around is deep, absolute. Not a shard of light is present in this new existence.

Nor is there any movement. My body is paralyzed, both inside and out.

I can't feel my toes or fingers. I can't part my lips to speak. I can't peel my eyes open to see. Even my ears seem closed off to any sounds.

My chest lies still. I have no heartbeat. Fitting, as I am drained dry. There is nothing inside of me that needs to move around.

Not blood. Not air.

I am dead.

I don't like that thought. I don't want to be dead. Not yet. There is something I must do before I die.

With that thought, I feel a twitch. Just a tiny stirring down below. Barely a blip on the radar of what's left of my consciousness. It's enough to warrant notice.

I can't lift my head to see what is touching me. I couldn't open my eyes even if I were able to. I can't defend myself if I have to.

The stirring becomes movement. Still only a slight shifting. But there is definitely something perched on my skin. My upper leg, I think?

Whatever the creature is, it leaves behind a wet trail on my cool skin as it progresses onward. Perhaps it's a worm?

No, not a worm. I'm starting to perceive girth as I differentiate its heat from my balmy flesh. Maybe a snake?

But no. It's not a snake. I can't perceive any scales as it continues to writhe on me.

The movements are definitely snake-like. Not a garden variety snake. Much more like…

Like an anaconda.

Awareness flashes at me in the darkness. A tiny pinpoint of light.

"Frankie?"

My words are not spoken out loud. They're said in my head. They're spoken in her voice.

Zahara called my cock *Frankie* on more than one occasion. I remember now. She thought I would put Frankie into another woman. Her wee claws had come out at the possibility. Fire had flashed in her cat eyes.

That light flashes in my mind now. I can't make out her features. But I know she is that light.

Down below, Frankie pulses again, as though he knows the light in my mind is the only woman he has ever craved. The only woman who has ever brought us both any pleasure. The woman who brought me and my dick together in the same body.

I wasn't able to get it up for two centuries. Not until Zahara came close and shone her bright light upon me.

But if Frankie is getting hard, maybe she is around?

As if in answer, my cock pulses again. It's only a light pulse, likely because there's barely a drop of blood in me. And anything I have is being diverted down south.

I'm going to need some of that blood diverted back up top. I need to think. If she is nearby, I need to get to her. I need a plan.

If only Gaius were here. He is the thinker in the family.

"If my brother is dead, I'm going to have myself a new jaguar coat."

The threat is said in Gaius's cultured voice, though it's gruffer than I've heard in decades. It harkens back to his street thug days.

"Gaius, that is really culturally insensitive; threatening to take the—well, fur—of a Native American shape-shifter. Or, wait? Is it Amerindian? Or maybe American Natives? I don't think we learned about indigenous people further south than Mexico in school?"

That's Cari's voice. For the short time that she's been in our family, she's been trying to help me with my clothing. Apparently, sometimes the way I dress is offensive to others.

"My apologies if I was offensive in threatening to do bodily harm to the elderly female jaguar shifter who staked and bled my brother to a painful, gruesome, and bloody death. Is that polite enough for you?"

"Well," says Cari in the patient voice she uses with me when I've gotten something wrong, "you didn't need to bring up her age."

"Shut it, both of you! I don't have time to deal with your colonizer-guilt."

Zahara's voice washes over me like sunlight. She sounds closer than the others. She sounds like she is a star just over my head. I want to reach out and touch her.

"Not a colonist," huffs Gaius, his cultured Italian firmly back in place.

"Second-generation French-American," mumbles Cari, with a soft lilt to her words.

There's a part of me that wants to point a finger at their flubs. Usually, I'm the one saying the wrong thing and causing discomfort to others. Unfortunately, I still can't lift a hand or open my mouth.

"Viri, can you hear me?" says Zahara.

Words bubble in my throat with no way to escape.

I try to part my lips. They don't budge.

I try to open my eyes. The lids are heavier than boulders.

I try to lift my hands towards her, but even if I could move, I'm not sure where to reach. The darkness cloaks me. Its cold tendrils snake under me. They close around me, like a mighty anaconda readying to suck the life out of me.

"Viri, I need you to open your eyes."

I want to. Fates, do I want to see her face again. I want the bright light of her gaze to warm me from this bitter cold.

"I need you to come back to me, Viri."

I want to tell her that I'll never leave her. Even if I must leave this world, my ghost will haunt her. I am the moth. She is the flame. If I die, it will be because her light burned me up.

"Viri, I love you."

My brothers had tried to explain how powerful those three words were. They had only ever been letters to me, and I was never good with my letters. The statement is made up of vowels, giving them a soft sound.

Those three syllables land heavily on my ears. They sink into my heart with a thud. They fill my lungs with a whisper of air. They move the dark clouds from behind my eyelids. I know my eyes are still closed, but on the other side of my lids, I begin to see the light.

The hardest part is lifting my eyelashes from their resting place on my cheekbones. It takes all my might to raise them just a fraction. But it's enough. Through the hairline bars of my jail cell, I see the light dawning.

I see the bright beam of light that is Zahara. I reach for the light.

CHAPTER 29

ZAHARA

*H*e's still. He's so very, very still.

I watched Virius in his daytime coma-like sleep more than once. His chest always rose and fell—eventually. His nostrils always flared with the intake of breath—eventually. His arms would come around me and pull me close to him—always.

Looking down at him, I see he is pale, lifeless. His chest is sunken in. His proud nose looks as though it has collapsed. His arms are inanimate objects at his sides that do not rise to take hold of me.

"Viri, can you hear me?"

I wrap my arms around him. He is cold to the touch. Not like ice. More like that flabby cold when a limb goes numb. I rub his skin vigorously, trying to get warmth back into him.

"Viri, I need you to open your eyes."

There is a flutter of movement. Not in his eyes. I turn my gaze away from his face and look southward.

Yes, there it is again. Movement in his pants. The front of his pants writhes and coils slowly, like a snake.

It's Frankie. Frankie is alive and well. That has to mean Viri is, too.

"I need you to come back to me, Viri." I place my hand on his groin. It pulses under my touch. But only once. Still, it's enough to let me know he's there.

A gasp goes through the gathered shifters and vampires. I don't care what they think. I only care about him, and if this will stir him enough to bring him back to me, then so be it.

"Viri, I love you."

"He needs blood," says Gaius. "We need to get him home and get him a blood bag."

A growl rips through the cave. The sound is so terrible and fearsome that every shifter—including Itzel, who is in Hadrian's grasp—drops lower and shows their neck. I look around for the source of the monster, only to realize the roar came from me.

"He drinks no one but me," I say before tearing a fang into my wrist.

Another gasp goes through the gathered shifters as my blood drips onto Virius's lips. I pull his lips apart to get more of my life-giving essence inside of him. Hell, I'll rip open my heart if it will bring him back to me.

His lips wrap around my wrist. The tip of his tongue slides across the slit of my wrist. Its velvety smoothness against the flesh of my veins is just as erotic as when he suckled on my intimate flesh. It's more satisfying because it's a sign of life.

And then, finally, he pulls.

His chest rises. His nostrils flare. His hand rises, and he presses my wrist to his mouth.

His eyes do not open. However, he continues to pull from me.

"Viri, that's enough," says Gaius.

He doesn't hear, or he doesn't listen. He pulls again.

"That's not what's supposed to happen," says Itzel. "That bloodsucker is going to kill her. They both need to live, for the child."

I want to laugh at her protests. If I do decide to have a child, it will not be born with a job. It will not be born shackled to a fate it has no control over, like both its parents.

That's only if we both live. Because if Virius doesn't come back into the light, I will live the rest of my life in complete darkness. How could I not, when he was my source of warmth?

But it would seem that will not be my fate. It will not be our fate.

Virius will not die. I feel that as he pulls at me again. I feel my life going into him, bringing him back to life. In return, I feel myself dimming ever so slightly.

One more pull, and I'm sure I will faint. I don't try to tug my hand away. I don't try to stop him.

I had planned to take his life from this man. But in the short days that I've known him, he's given me a reason to truly live. If this is the cost, I'll pay it. I'll give him my life.

I take a deep breath, likely the last one I'll ever take, and wait for the next pull.

Viri's eyes flash open. They are no longer dark. They flash back at me, like a cat's.

His smile is bloody. "There you are."

"There you are," I whisper as I press my forehead against his.

"Everything went dark all around me. But then there was a tiny spark of light. It was you. You are my sun. You've set me free."

I cup his cheek in my hand. The warmth is returning to him now that my blood is in his veins. He is alive. Like, truly alive. That metallic note of vampire is fading from his skin. Not entirely, but mostly.

"What will become of the prophecy?"

I raise my head to see Itzel. Gaius's hold on her hasn't slipped. She doesn't appear to care about her life. All she's ever cared about is the damn gods, not the flesh and blood woman that I am.

"As I told my mate, prophecies are rarely what they seem," says Virius, his voice still reedy from his near death. "But with this one, it looks like everyone got what they came for. So we'll call it even. Let her go, brother."

Gaius's fingers twitch around Itzel's neck. He takes in a deep breath. Then he looks at me. He's giving me the choice.

"It's your land," Gaius says. "They're your people. It's your say."

I don't hesitate. I know exactly what I want to do. I turn to the women who have been there all my life. They raised me to think I was something special. They taught me to fight, to take care of myself. But they never allowed me to define my own destiny.

"Go home."

A bristle runs through the crowd, much like a cat who's had her fur rubbed the wrong way. My words aren't directed at the crowd. They're directed at Itzel.

"I've listened to your words all my life," I say. "And they nearly killed me, and the man I love."

I look to Viri, who has sat up on the makeshift altar. The wounds on his chest and wrist are healing slowly. Not as fast as they would normally, but I can see that his life is no longer in jeopardy.

"I think this prophecy was meant to bring us together. All of us." I look around the room at the shifters and vampires under one roof. Or, rather, one cave. "You're the only one who tried to tear us apart."

Gaius shifts his hold on Itzel. His face contorts with guilt. "You," I say to him, "I think you'll come around."

He raises a brow, and then sighs in a reluctant sound of agreement.

I turn to the rest of the women gathered. "You all have a choice of what path you'll follow. You can either stay here and build this community. Or you can go back to the old ways with her. It's your choice, which is more than I ever got."

I don't wait to see what choices get made. I only care to focus on one person's wellbeing. Viri has to lean on me and my strength as we walk out of the cave. But I barely feel his weight as Gaius is at his side, Hadrian is at his back, and Cari's hand is in mine.

This is my new family. They aren't perfect. They're a little crazy. But they have accepted me with no strings or prophecies attached, so it's an improvement.

I tuck my head under Viri's chin. I can hear his heart beating in his chest. His breath ruffles my hair. His strong arms are around me, holding me tight, and letting me know he'll never let me go.

EPILOGUE

VIRIUS

The rays on my face warm me from the tip of my nose on down to my toes. I'm barefoot as I stand in the sunlight, waiting for it to set as I wait for my mate.

"You're going to roast if you don't come into the shade."

My nose wrinkles, more at the smell of the lotion full of SPF than at Hadrian's voice. Some of my supernatural powers stayed with me when my blood was drained.

I am still abnormally strong, but I think that has more to do with my genes than anything else. I am still fast, though now everyone in my family could outpace me. Everyone except Marechal, who is the last remaining human hold out.

I can walk in the sun now, though I still would burn. Just not to a crisp like other vampires. Because I'm not exactly a vampire anymore. Nor am I a shifter. I'm also not exactly human.

But my skin will sunburn if I don't protect it. Already

there is a red splotch on my forearm. So I heed my brother's words and step back inside the kitchen as the sun sets.

Hadrian isn't standing at the glass of the door, glaring at the solar orb like he's done every dusk for the last two hundred years. Instead, my vampire brother is at the stove, cooking a meaty dish in a wine reduction. It's wine from this year's harvest of the Balam Vineyards. The first year's vintage was in such high demand that the jaguar shifters working the land are now well into selling next year's crops.

Outside, the men and women of the Balam shifters come out of their homes and start the nightly ritual of tending to the vines which will secure their families' futures.

"Come away from the door," says Hadrian as he flips the meatballs. "She won't get here any faster with the screen open."

I give the long driveway one last lingering look. If she's more than a few yards away, I won't be able to hear her. My vampiric sense has deadened, but my hearing has grown sharper than ever. The crunch of gravel from a mile down the road tells me she's almost home.

"Ah, brother, you're making my favorite." Gaius appears in the doorway to the kitchen. The silk robe he wears is easily worth more than the grapes brought in this harvest. *"Animelles."*

Hadrian smacks Gaius's hand with the prongs before he can snag one of the fried testicles from the hot pan. "I thought it fitting, as this is the anniversary of our first year here."

"One year," muses Gaius. "Hard to believe, as so much has changed."

Everything had changed. This land is no longer ours. We're guests in our own house. But not one of us has any inclination to leave. Not when our mates love the land.

157

That is the most important change. We are all happily mated. And not one of our mates is psychotic or sadistic.

"You've got some balls on you, honey," says Cari as she comes up behind Hadrian.

"They're Gaius's favorite."

"I'm not eating that," says Marechal as she makes her way to the sink to wash the soil from her hands.

"You eat frog legs and snails," protests Gaius.

"You really want me to put another man's balls in my mouth?"

"It's a bull," he says, kissing her neck and then staring at the vein of her jugular. "It's like eating a hamburger."

I ignore the jibes between the two couples as a car comes to a stop in the driveway. I step outside into the moonlight as my own personal sun rises from the driver's seat of the Tesla. It was a mighty task trying to get my wee kitten to spend the money I signed over to her, but she got the hang of it pretty quickly.

My eyes latch onto the six-inch heels that hug her slender feet. I'm already peeling the designer jeans from that lush ass with my mind. She flashes those sharp canines at me as I prowl up to her.

"There's my strong Roman," she purrs as I scoop her into my embrace.

I take her lips in greeting. My salutation is to slip my tongue into her mouth. My fangs are still there, but they're not as sharp as they once were. They are sharp enough to nick her tongue.

I lap up the droplet of blood I find there. I don't need much blood these days. But Zahara's essence is still an addiction.

"Guess who's the only student who got a hundred percent on her midterm?" she says when I release her lips.

"I don't need to guess," I say, carrying her out of the driveway and into the house.

"Hey, Z."

"Good day at school?"

"We're sitting down to eat in thirty, you two."

Zahara can't answer any of our family members with my tongue back in her mouth. I feel her hand leave my back as she waves a greeting to them. Then she yelps when I toss her onto our bed.

"You're being rude," she says after bouncing on the bed.

"I'm having dessert first," I say, unbuckling my pants.

"You'll ruin your appetite," she says while slipping out of her own jeans.

"Nah, I think I'll whet it," I say as I spread her thighs.

The flesh I find there is already flushed and red. Without preamble, I take her bud into my mouth. Zahara digs her claws into my hair as she presses me to her.

I lick and lave her pretty pussy until she trembles not once, but twice. Before she comes down from her second orgasm, I sink my fangs into my favorite of her femoral arteries.

Zahara howls as I gulp down a mouthful of her sweet, rich, endorphin-laced blood. A third orgasm rips through her as I suck. Her friend Frankie pulses with impatience for his turn.

He'll have to wait until I've strapped him up. We're pretty certain that getting Zahara pregnant is now one of my super-powers. But we've decided to wait, at least until after Zahara finishes university. Maybe longer.

It doesn't matter, the length of time. Though I know I gave up an eternal lifetime for her, I don't doubt for a second that every moment with her and with the child we will share someday will be worth every century I'll miss.

I take Frankie in hand as I prowl up her body. Zahara is

blissed out from her three climaxes. I ease my way into her tight sheath. As always, it's a tight fit. But my woman, my mate, is eager to take all of me. And not just the part that is crazy about her.

She takes all of me, as I take all of her. She is the light that led me out of the darkness. It is for her that I came back to life after centuries of being the walking dead. It is because of her that I now truly live. Because, being with her, I am finally free.

The End

Want more vampire romance by Ines Johnson?
Read Arneis Durand's story where he meets, makes love to, and falls in love with -yes, in that order- a vampire princess in His Vampire Princess, available exclusively in the All Souls' Night anthology!

WANT MORE MIDNIGHT DOMS?

Click here to sign up for news!

Read the whole series for more of your favorite vampire BDSM club:

Alpha's Blood by Renee Rose & Lee Savino

Her Vampire Master by Maren Smith

Her Vampire Prince by Ines Johnson

Her Vampire Hero by Nicolina Martin

Her Vampire Bad Boy by Brenda Trim

Her Vampire Rebel by Zara Zenia

Her Vampire Obsession by Tymber Dalton, writing as Lesli Richardson

Her Vampire Temptation by Alexis Alvarez

Her Vampire Addiction by Tabitha Black

Her Vampire Lord by Ines Johnson

Her Vampire Suspect by Brenda Trim

His Captive Mortal by Renee Rose & Lee Savino

The Vampire's Captive by Kay Elle Parker

The Vampire's Prey - Vivian Murdoch

All Souls' Night - A Midnight Doms Anthology

Her Vampire Assassin - Erin St. Charles

Her Vampire Knight -Ines Johnson

ABOUT THE AUTHOR

Lover of fairytales, folklore, and mythology, Ines Johnson spends her days reimagining the stories of old in a modern world. She writes books where damsels cause the distress, princesses wield swords, and moms save the world.

If you liked Ines' Vampires, then you'll love her Dragons, alpha male shifters, fated mates, and steamy romance with a touch of 80's nostalgia! To grab a free book from the world of the Last Dragons just visit https://ineswrites.com/ReaderGroup

CPSIA information can be obtained
at www.ICGtesting.com
Printed in the USA
LVHW051443240422
717084LV00004B/514